CI7

CW01090848

'Beautifully written; sophisticated, sensitive and dealing with huge themes with such a lightness of touch'

LAURA DOCKRILL

'A sweet story of family, acceptance – and horses!'

JO COTTERILL

'A sweet novel that deals with grief, unemployment, moving home, secrets, fear and standing up for what's right in such a beautiful and honest way. Any horse lovers out there will adore this!'

TAMSIN WINTER

'A heart-warming story of friendship, family and overcoming new challenges... with added ponies!'

CATHY CASSIDY

FRANCES MOLONEY was born and raised in London, where she now lives having spent brief stints in Cornwall, where she studied English with Creative Writing at Falmouth, and Sweden. She has worked in the world of stories for over ten years and loves reading, running and yoga – though not all at the same time! Frances's debut novel, *The Mystery of the Missing Mum*, is also available from Pushkin Children's.

CITY OF HORSES

FRANCES MOLONEY

PUSHKIN CHILDREN'S

Pushkin Press
Somerset House, Strand
London WC2R 1LA

First published by Pushkin Press in 2023

1 3 5 7 9 8 6 4 2

ISBN 13: 978-1-78269-396-3

Designed and typeset by Tetragon, London

Printed and bound by Clays Ltd, Elcograf S.p.A.

www.pushkinpress.com

For my dad, the best muck sweeper in town!

CHAPTER ONE

It was the first day of the winter term, and the sky was grey and blustery as Misty made her way towards the school gates. Her pace quickened as she approached, the anticipation of seeing her two closest friends after what had felt like, to her, a never-ending break, building with every step that she took.

It wasn't that she couldn't wait to tell them about all the exciting things she had done with her time off, it was in fact the exact opposite, she couldn't wait to forget about it entirely. The holiday had dragged. Misty had spent most of it curled up on the sofa, scrolling mindlessly through channels on the TV. Her father had tried his best to fill the void left in her life since her mother had died the summer before Misty started secondary school, but his idea of a Christmas dinner consisted of a plate of sausage rolls and readymade roast potatoes that were on offer in ALDI.

When Misty's mum was still alive, Christmases had bristled with excitement. A few weeks before the big day, her dad would bring home a real, six-foot-tall fir tree, which Misty and her mum would decorate carefully with the baubles they had collected; one for each year since Misty was born. Her dad would be in charge of the music, Slade and Paul McCartney's cheesy festive tunes blasting out of the antiquated CD player that perched in the corner of the living room like a relic from a previous life. Misty hadn't minded her dad's retro music taste so much back then. Back when there were still three of them and everything was generally much easier to tolerate.

Misty could barely remember her first Christmas without her mother. That year had passed by in a numbing blur; there were no forced celebrations, just an empty space where the tree would normally be, an aching reminder of all they had lost. She wasn't sure which had been worse, the complete absence of the past two years, forgetting about it altogether, or the fake festivities of this most recent Christmas. Either way, she couldn't wait to see her friends and go back to the safety and security of the regular school routine.

As usual, despite living the nearest to school, Misty was the last of her friends to arrive. Ruby's mum was a successful lawyer who always dropped off Ruby well before school started and Jasmine, Misty's other best friend, just didn't like being late for anything. Misty was by far the most disorganised of the trio, always joining them at the last minute, her fiery red hair streaming out behind her, papers escaping from the top of her rucksack where she had hastily stuffed them before leaving the house.

It hadn't always been this way but without her mother to remind her to pack her school bag the night before, handing her a lunchbox on her way out the door and asking if she had her PE kit, it wasn't so easy. Her dad was too busy trying to hold down a job, run the house and pay for everything on one salary, so Misty tried her best not to bother him with anything she considered too trivial. Secondary school had offered Misty a fresh start. It was a chance to make new friends in a place where she wasn't defined by or reminded of her loss.

As she passed through the gates and entered the playground, Misty made her way over to her friends. She was relieved to find that they weren't talking about the Christmas break at all. Ruby was clutching an A5 piece of paper tightly to her chest and gesturing animatedly in Jasmine's direction, barely pausing to acknowledge Misty as she approached them. Ruby was the confident one, which meant the other Year Nine girls were secretly a little bit afraid of her. She had wild curly black hair and olive-toned skin.

'Auditions start this week,' Ruby exclaimed in excitement, without giving any additional context. 'The first round are at lunchtime.'

'Auditions for what?' Misty asked, her brain struggling to click into gear.

'For the school play, silly,' Ruby replied, as if this was the densest question she had ever had the misfortune to answer. 'It's *Romeo and Juliet* this year and I'm going to play Juliet.'

'If you get the part,' Jasmine suggested timidly. She stood literally head and shoulders above all of the other girls in their year and spent most of her time trying and failing to blend into the background. Her white-blonde hair and elvish pale skin didn't help much.

'Of course I will. Look, I've been practising.' Ruby mimed drawing a dagger over her throat in a very dramatic fashion.

'I thought she poisoned herself?' Misty asked distractedly.

'She did but it didn't work. That was Romeo,' Ruby continued. 'Then Juliet wakes up, finds him dead and stabs herself. It's all very complicated, you see. And *very* romantic. Can you imagine wanting to kill yourself over Shaun in Year Eleven?'

'I think she stabs herself in the side.' Jasmine blushed as she tried to steer the conversation away from the mention of her crush. The girls had been studying the Shakespeare play in their English class the previous term.

'I know,' Ruby confirmed. 'I just decided that doing it this way would have more impact. You could call it artistic license, I suppose.'

'I'm sure you'll get the part,' Misty said firmly.

The sound of the bell cut through Ruby's reply and the three girls headed off towards their form groups for registration. Misty and Jasmine were both in the same form, 9C, but Ruby was in 9E, much to her annoyance. Even Ruby couldn't persuade the teachers to move her to the same form as her friends.

'Good luck!' Misty called as Ruby turned and marched off in the opposite direction, practising her lines as she went. 'See you later.'

But Ruby didn't reply for she was already busy, lost in her own world of plays and poetry, imagining what it would feel like to lose her imaginary lover to his own fatal hand.

'How were the auditions?' Misty asked when she met Ruby in the playground after school. Jasmine had already left for her after-school swimming lesson, but Misty had stayed behind knowing that Ruby would be raring to give her a full, blow-by-blow account of the proceedings.

'Fine,' Ruby replied hesitantly. 'At least, I *think* I did enough to impress them.'

'I'm sure you did.'

'They told me I got through to the next round anyway, though I was kind of hoping they'd be so blown away by my performance they would offer me the part of Juliet on the spot.'

'When is the next round?' Usually, the main part in the school play went to one of the older pupils in the school but Misty was used to Ruby's outlandish imaginings and knew it was usually best to go along with them. Besides, if anyone could defeat the Year Eleven girls, Ruby would be the one to do it.

'Wednesday and we'll find out who got what part on Friday. They're going to put a list up on the noticeboard outside the Year Eleven common room.'

The girls turned at the sound of a roaring engine as a sleek four-by-four drew up alongside them. Ruby's younger brother, Jason, was hanging out of the back window pulling faces at them as her mum shouted for Ruby to get in the car.

'I'd better go,' Ruby said glumly. 'See you tomorrow.'

As Ruby opened the door on the front passenger side, Misty could see that her mum was busy taking a call on her hands-free and already indicating, impatient to be off as she tried to pull out into the busy after-school traffic.

'Sorry, Misty,' Ruby's mum called out of the window. 'I'd give you a lift home, but I've got to get back for a meeting.'

'That's ok, Sheila. Bye, Ruby. See you tomorrow,' she called as the car edged its way slowly forward. She smiled wistfully as the vehicle retreated, missing the hustle and bustle of her friend's family already.

*

As Misty walked up the hill towards home, she could see that all of the lights were on in the living room even though it was only four o'clock in the afternoon. The house glowed ominously in the cold, winter darkness like a lighthouse warning her to stay away from the door. From the top of the hill, you could almost make out the hidden blackness of the sea in the distance, and a sudden chill made her pause for a moment, before pushing on through the downward gusts of wind and upwards to where the house was waiting to greet her.

Misty pushed open the cast-iron gate and it squeaked in protest as she dislodged droplets of frozen water from its hinges. The path was overgrown with weeds, but the lawn was as immaculate as ever and there didn't seem to be any other sign of a disturbance. The door stood closed before her, its bright red paint a cheerful contrast to the surrounding gloom. The windows were tightly shut to keep the cool evening air at bay. From the front garden, the living room looked undisturbed.

Misty opened the front door and stepped quietly into the tiled hallway. The first thing she noticed was her dad's waterproof jacket, hanging on the coat rack in the hall. She was at once comforted by its familiar shape and smell and confused as to why it was there at all. It was far too early for her dad to be home from work, and he wouldn't have gone out into the sharp, crisp air that morning without it.

She shrugged off her own coat and pulled off her fur-lined boots and left them in an ungainly pile at the foot of the stairs.

She followed the beacon of bulbs that lit the way to the kitchen like a string of clues that had been left for her to follow. It was in the kitchen that she found her dad, a steaming mug of tea before him. He sat hunched over the old oak table, the opposite of his usual cheerful demeanour, his hands clasped tightly around the tea as if it would get up and walk away if he let go.

'Dad?' Misty must have said his name thousands if not millions of times before but this time it sounded more like a question than an answer. Her dad didn't move, couldn't seem to tear his eyes away from the milky film that was appearing on the top of his drink.

'Dad?' she called again, trying to keep the rising note of panic out of her voice. 'Dad, is everything ok?'

It had just been Misty and her father for the past two and a half years. Things hadn't always been easy between them, but they had eventually settled into a new routine that now felt like a comfy pair of slippers. They were moulded to each other, almost inseparable. This new silent man wasn't anything like Misty's real father. She didn't recognise him at all.

Just when Misty had almost given up hope of him answering, her dad turned his gaze towards her. He looked slightly older and more wrinkled than he had that morning, but behind the worry in his eyes she could see a reassuring flicker of the dad she remembered. He must still be in there somewhere.

'What's happened? Please tell me what's wrong?'

Her dad looked at her, confused for a moment as if he didn't recognise that the thirteen-year-old girl stood before him was, in fact, his own daughter. His eyes sought out her own and, in that moment, he seemed to remember who he was, who she was.

'Misty,' he said, breaking out of his stupor as quickly as it had come upon him. 'How was school today?' His voice was still much the same as she remembered, though the lyrical vowels were perhaps a little hoarser sounding than normal.

'School?' Misty replied, as if she too had temporarily forgotten herself. 'Fine. Fine, but—'

'That's good to hear.' Dad got up and poured the untouched cup of tea down the sink as if nothing had happened. The brown liquid splashed untidily over the cool porcelain.

'Dad, why are you home so early?' Misty asked, hoping for a response.

Her father was usually a hive of bustling activity, asking her how her day was, if she needed any help with her homework, what she and her friends were up to that weekend, all whilst chopping onions for dinner, trying not to let them make him cry (the onions always won in the end), and putting on a wash at the same time. It was exhausting just watching him.

'Misty, there's something you should know.'

Misty suddenly felt exhaustion of an entirely different kind. It was the type that tiptoes up behind you unexpectedly and drains the life out of your very bones. It was the feeling of dread. It was quietly creeping up her spine and making all the hairs on her entire body stand fiercely to attention and her heart pound. It was preparing her for bad news.

'They've let me go.'

For a second, Misty wondered what her father meant. *Let him go where?* She briefly thought it was a positive statement: *They've let me go... on holiday... to the beach... away somewhere hot and sunny.* But this was an old mining community, and almost everyone knew what it meant to simply be swept away like discarded rubbish and then entirely forgotten about. And now Misty's father knew too, had been given first-hand experience of it.

'Why?' Misty asked, her mouth hanging open in shock. Her dad had worked for the same firm for over ten years, he was one of their top accountants. Whenever Misty met his boss, Mr Peters, he always told her that her dad was 'one of Gold Star's most valuable assets' whilst chuckling merrily to himself and patting Misty on the head as if she was forever three years old.

'The company's been having some financial problems. They need to get rid of a few people. Those people include me,' he said bitterly.

'I'm sorry, Dad, I'm sure you'll find another job soon.'

The clichés started pouring out of Misty without her having to think about it. Things she'd heard other people say, things she thought you were meant to say to someone who had just lost their work. It wasn't as if he had momentarily misplaced it, she thought. That he could find it again, if only he looked hard enough.

'I'm sure something will come up,' she continued. 'We'll manage.'

'Thanks, love.'

'Perhaps I can find a weekend job?' she offered halfheartedly. She didn't suppose anyone would allow a thirteen-year-old to work for them. 'I could wash cars for the neighbours or walk their dogs or something—'

'I'm sure it won't come to that, I'll get something else sorted out,' Dad interrupted her mid-flow, and she felt suddenly relieved and then, just as quickly, selfish for feeling that way after everything he had done for her.

'We'll get by, right enough.'

CHAPTER TWO

The next morning, Misty got herself up and ready for school as normal. As she dressed and brushed her teeth, the door to her father's bedroom stayed firmly shut, and she didn't stop to try and work out whether he was inside it or not. She tried not to think about how it had been after her mum had died, when her dad struggled to get out of bed for weeks. Instead, she crept silently down the carpeted stairs and into the kitchen below. The clean countertops sparkled brightly in the winter morning sunlight as if nothing out of the ordinary had happened the night before. Misty made herself a bowl of cereal and poured a glass of orange juice, chewing and swallowing as if on autopilot.

As soon as she left the house, the cold, sharp sea breeze hit her straight in the face and whipped her hair into a frenzy. By the time she arrived at the school gates, Misty had already decided that she wasn't going to tell anyone what had happened to her father – not even Ruby and Jasmine. She told herself that her dad would find work soon and no one would ever need to know. She wasn't going to lie to anyone directly, she was merely withholding the truth until everything was sorted and then it would be irrelevant anyway.

The playground was filled with small huddles of chatty teenage girls and overgrown boys kicking footballs back and forth to one another. Misty walked quickly towards the science block, sidestepping the speeding balls as she went, to where she usually met her friends. Having smoothed down her hair, her hands now grasped the straps of her backpack tightly as she marched across the crowded concrete. The sea of bodies parted to let her through like a wave pulling back from the shore.

'Misty, over here!' shouted Ruby.

'Hi Ruby! Hi Jasmine!' Misty called out to her friends.

'Hi Misty,' Jasmine replied, as considered and calm as ever, even amidst a sea of playground excitement.

'Do you want to come to mine after school?' Ruby cut straight to the chase as usual. 'I need help practising for the final auditions tomorrow.'

Her friends were leaning against the wall of the ugly, nineteen seventies-style science building. Misty looked up at its identical set of rectangular windows, which seemed to stare down at her as she tried to think of an excuse.

'I'm not sure I can tonight.' Misty didn't want to leave her dad on his own for too long and she knew if she went round to Ruby's, her friends would easily spot that something was on her mind.

'Oh, right.' Ruby looked slightly taken aback. She was used to getting her own way and didn't like it when things didn't go to plan.

Jasmine watched the pair of them and Misty knew she was hoping there wasn't going to be an argument. She hated it when they fell out.

'I'll help you, Ruby,' Jasmine offered quietly, doing her best to smooth things over. 'I'm sure you don't need both of us to watch.'

'Thanks, Jasmine. I promised Dad I'd help him with something.' Misty decided it was best to stick as close to the truth as possible, her dad did need her after all. It was only a small, white lie. Hopefully Ruby was too busy thinking about her rehearsals for the audition and she wouldn't see straight through it.

Ruby looked as though she was about to ask Misty what she was meant to be helping with but luckily, just as she opened her mouth to speak, the bell started ringing, signalling that it was time for registration.

'I'll see you later, Jasmine,' Ruby called as she headed towards the older part of the school where the Art and English buildings were. Ruby had drama club at lunchtime so they wouldn't even have a chance to see each other until the end of the day, which was probably for the best.

'See you then!' Jasmine replied.

'I hope she's not annoyed with me,' Misty confessed once Ruby had rushed off. 'You know what she can be like sometimes.'

'Don't worry,' Jasmine replied conspiratorially. 'She'll get over it.'

The girls hurried inside. Once registration was over, Misty and Jasmine went their separate ways for their first lessons. Misty spent the rest of the day trying to act as if nothing out of the ordinary was happening whilst also trying to avoid bumping into either of her friends, which was far from normal and was bound to raise their suspicions. At breaktime she went straight to the library, on the pretence of having to look for a new book to read and she spent her lunchbreak catching up on the homework she hadn't had time to complete the previous evening.

Once school was over, she left quickly, without waiting to say goodbye. Even as she rushed up the hill towards home, she could hear her phone vibrating busily in her coat pocket, probably with messages from Ruby and Jasmine asking why she had left in such a hurry. She had told them that she wasn't free, she thought irritably, why couldn't they just drop it?

This time when Misty arrived home, the house was still in darkness. She turned on the overhead hallway lights which cast a welcoming glow down the hallway as she walked towards the empty kitchen. Misty flicked the switch on the kettle with fingers still clumsy from cold and waited patiently as a comforting bubbling sound filled the silence.

'Dad?' she called from the bottom of the stairs, where she hovered hesitantly with two cups brimming with tea. She cocked her head slightly, her ear raised towards the ceiling like a spaniel eager for its owner's command. When there was no response, she stepped tentatively up the stairs, pausing to set down one of the cups on the top of the banister whilst she tapped softly on her father's closed bedroom door.

'Come in,' called a gruff voice and Misty pushed the door open wide. 'Sorry, I lost track of the time.'

'I've made tea,' Misty said as she took in the chaos of the room. The bed was made, much to her relief, but it was covered in papers. Her dad was sitting in the corner of the room in front of his computer, a silhouette in the early evening gloom.

'I've been doing job applications,' he said determinedly, gesturing to the mess surrounding him. 'Might as well start straightaway.'

'Do you need any help?' Misty wasn't sure what use she would be, but she could definitely make a start on the clearing up.

'No, no, that's ok love, I'm almost done for today. Why don't you go downstairs and watch telly? I'll be down in a minute. I'll make us something to eat.'

An hour later, Misty was huddled on the sofa reading a book when she heard the clatter of pots and pans coming from the kitchen. The radio was on, and she could hear her dad humming absentmindedly as he prepared dinner. *Perhaps nothing will have to change after all?* Misty thought. She snuggled down further beneath her blanket and started to doze contentedly, surrounded by the familiar sounds of her everyday routine. Her dad seemed certain that it wouldn't take him very long to get a new job and Misty was reassured to see that he was approaching the search with his typical positivity.

Just as she was about to fall asleep, Misty's phone buzzed aggressively, jolting her back into wakefulness. It was a video of Ruby rehearsing Juliet's final soliloquy and Misty speedily sent a row of three thumbs-up emojis in reply. She was going to have to think of a convincing explanation for her absence when they asked; it wasn't as if she could tell them she had been helping her dad with job applications all evening.

'Dinner's ready!' Dad shouted from the kitchen.

'Coming.' Misty took one last glance at her phone and shoved it hurriedly down the back of the sofa cushions.

The kitchen smelled of a comforting mixture of Italian herbs and warm tomato sauce as Misty's dad spooned large portions of pasta into two bowls that were set out on the table in front of him.

'Thanks Dad, this looks great,' Misty said as she sat down, her stomach rumbling in agreement. Although her dad's cooking was basic and he mainly stuck to simple dishes like pasta sauces and stew, it generally tasted pretty good.

'See, everything will be just fine,' her dad answered, pouring himself a glass of wine and Misty some water from a glass jug that had once been one of her mother's most prized possessions.

Misty smiled, a mouthful of delicious food making it impossible for her to respond. And in that tranquil moment, just an everyday dinner at the kitchen table, with her belly completely stuffed, Misty believed every word. She didn't even stop for a moment to wonder if what her father was saying was true. It was impossible for her to imagine that things might be about to transform completely, irrevocably, and forever.

CHAPTER THREE

'I got the part!' Ruby screamed triumphantly. It was Friday morning breaktime and Misty had raced downstairs as soon as class was over to find out if the audition had been a success. Ruby had been so caught up in her preparation for the past couple of days that it had been easy enough for Misty to blend seamlessly into the background, but she knew her best friend would notice if she wasn't there waiting to celebrate or commiserate with her.

'I knew you could do it!' Misty exclaimed, ignoring the looks of disdain some of the Year Eleven girls were throwing their way. 'Ignore them, they're just jealous.'

'I can't believe it.' Misty needn't have worried as Ruby continued obliviously. 'Me! Juliet!'

'Well done,' Jasmine chimed in as her head appeared above the crowd that were gathered in front of the noticeboard. She scanned the list of names eagerly until she found Ruby's. 'Look, there you are! Sorry I'm late, I had to speak to Mrs McIver about my chemistry homework.'

'That's ok,' Ruby replied. 'I couldn't have done it without your help... and my natural talent of course.'

'Maybe we should get out of here?' Misty suggested. Ruby's lack of tact was continuing to draw annoyed glances from the group of Year Eleven girls who had just found out they had missed out on the part of Juliet.

'I can't believe I got Lady Capulet,' one girl exclaimed, moodily tossing her long chestnut hair over her shoulder. 'She must be at least a hundred years old. I'm far too young to play that part.'

'Let's go outside,' Ruby agreed. 'We've not got long until breaktime's over and I want to know what you've been up to all week, Misty. You've been very quiet.' She shot her an accusing glare.

'Congratulations, Ruby,' called Ryan Bremer, saving Misty from having to come up with a convincing response and causing Ruby to turn the colour of a ripe tomato. 'See you in rehearsals on Monday.'

'He's playing Romeo,' Ruby whispered, almost swooning as the girls walked away. 'He's so good-looking. I can't believe I get to spend the whole term hanging out with him.'

'You're going to have so much fun,' Jasmine replied. 'I'm *almost* jealous.'

The three girls laughed knowing there was nothing Jasmine would hate more than being on stage in front of an enormous crowd. Even if Shaun Evans *was* playing Mercutio.

'It's certainly not for me,' Misty agreed. 'You couldn't pay me to get up on that stage either.'

'Hey—' Ruby started to protest.

'Don't worry. *You'll* be amazing. As you say, you're a pro and we'll be there cheering you on.'

'From the sidelines if that's ok?' Jasmine interjected. 'Just don't ask us to join in.'

'That's fine. I would never dream of it,' Ruby giggled, so swept up in her own excitement that she seemed to have completely forgotten about interrogating Misty. 'See you after school?'

The girls had arranged to have a sleepover at Ruby's that evening. They were having a film night and had been looking forward to it for ages, especially Jasmine who adored all things Disney and wasn't allowed to watch much TV at home. Her parents thought it was bad for the brain. Ruby's mum had got her a subscription to Disney+, so now they had unlimited access to all the films they wanted at the touch of a remote-controlled button.

'We'll be there,' Misty replied, feeling reassured after another uneventful evening at home that her father could cope without her for the night. 'Wouldn't miss it for the world.'

*

'So where *have* you been hiding?' Ruby asked Misty as soon as they got to her house that evening. Jasmine and Misty were lying on Ruby's bed watching as she set up Disney+ on her enormous TV.

'I've hardly been hiding,' Misty replied defensively. 'I told you I had to help my dad with something.'

Yes, but you've been very secretive about the whole thing,' Ruby persisted. 'Your dad doesn't usually ask you for help with anything. Usually, you're the one asking for *his* help.'

Although this wasn't strictly true, Misty hesitated for a moment, trying to think of a response that was convincing enough to throw Ruby off the scent but also so mundane it would stop her asking any more questions.

'He wanted... my opinion on paint colours. We're redecorating.' As she said it, she realised her mistake. Ruby was passionate about all things creative, and she liked art almost as much as she loved drama. At least it was somewhat plausible, her dad did like to ask her opinions on things now that it was just the two of them at home.

'Ohhh.' Ruby's eyes lit up with excitement. 'What did you go for in the end?'

'I'm not sure,' Misty mumbled. 'I mean, we haven't made a decision yet.'

'Well, if you need any help, you know where to come.'

'Can we order something to eat now?' Jasmine interrupted, pushing her glasses back up her nose. 'I'm starving.'

Jasmine was forever famished after all the sports that she played, and Ruby's mum always let them order whatever they wanted from Deliveroo, anything to save her from having to cook for them all.

'Let's see.' Ruby scrolled through the options on her smartphone. 'How about KFC? There's a deal on.'

'Sounds great,' Misty replied, relieved that the faux renovations seemed to have been forgotten, at least for the time being. She wasn't sure how she would explain the lack of a makeover in the future but that was a problem for another day.

Ruby paid with her mum's credit card; she had memorised the pin when she was six years old. Her friends always joked that she had come out of the womb knowing how to use online banking. Misty glanced towards the door where Ruby had set up an elaborate boobytrap to keep her little brother at bay. It consisted of several elastic bands, a chair that was wedged beneath the door handle, and a collection of precariously stacked exercise books.

'That should keep him out,' Ruby said smugly when she noticed where Misty was looking.

'I don't mind if he wants to join us,' Jasmine offered, as generous as ever.

'I know you don't mind but I do.' Ruby rolled her eyes. 'Last time I let Jason into my room he left horrible dirty handprints all over the walls. I don't know how he does it.'

Jasmine giggled. 'You realise we won't be able to get out either? What will we do when the food arrives? What if there's a fire?'

'Don't you worry, I have a cunning plan,' Ruby said vaguely. 'Just wait and see.'

After half an hour had passed, Ruby's phone screen lit up with the name of the delivery driver. 'I'll be right there,' Ruby said, grinning craftily as she answered it.

Luckily for Ruby, she lived in a one-storey new build, with large floor-to-ceiling windows in every room. As if he had done it a million times before, the driver's face appeared at the window directly opposite where they were sitting and Ruby pulled it open, collecting their bounty and saying 'thank you' to the driver all in one practised move.

'See, no need to leave this room,' Ruby said, glancing towards the ensuite bathroom in the corner.

'You certainly have everything we need,' Misty replied, trying to keep a hint of envy out of her voice.

'Come on. Less talking, more eating.' Jasmine was already opening the food containers impatiently. 'Mmm, this is delicious.'

Jasmine closed her eyes as she munched happily on a piece of fried chicken. Her parents were strict vegetarians and extremely health-conscious, so Jasmine used their sleepovers as an excuse to try different foods.

For the rest of the evening, they ate their meal, discussed Ruby's upcoming rehearsals, and watched Disney films in bed. Jasmine quietly let slip that she was training for a triathlon. Ruby was trying to think of reasons to spend more time alone with Ryan when Misty noticed that Jasmine was no longer talking. She was always the first to fall asleep, her body slowly slumping downwards until she was completely horizontal.

'Jasmine.' Ruby nudged her. 'You'll miss the end.'

'Numph,' Jasmine muttered incoherently, her eyelids closing as she spoke. 'I'm awake.'

'Some things never change.' Misty chuckled as she looked from one friend to the other. 'Night, Jasmine. Sleep tight.'

'Trust her to fall asleep during a film she picked.' Ruby rolled her eyes good-naturedly as she turned her attention back to the screen.

It wasn't long before Misty felt her own eyes grow heavy and she too was struggling to stay awake. When she glanced over, she noticed that Ruby's eyes were already shut, her face gently illuminated by the flickering images on the TV screen.

CHAPTER FOUR

It was during the February break that Misty's dad first mentioned the possibility of moving. The rest of the half term had passed swiftly, and Misty had been lulled into a false sense of security as she got wrapped up in Ruby's rehearsals for the school play and Jasmine's triathlon training and forgot about any problems she might be facing at home. She had been out shopping for the day in the centre of town with Ruby and Jasmine and she was still smiling as she walked through the front door and into the living room where her father was sitting at the coffee table with the newspaper spread out in front of him.

'It's only an option,' her dad said firmly, still staring dejectedly at the paper. 'It might not even come to it in the end. But if I don't find a job soon—'

'But where would we go?' Misty interrupted. 'This is our home. I don't want to live anywhere else.'

'Dave's got a house over in Redbridge. His parents' old place. It's just sitting empty, and he said we could stay there for a while. It would only be temporary. Just until we get back on our feet.'

Misty glanced down at her feet to make sure they were still firmly planted on the floor beneath her. *What about Mum?* she wanted to shout. Were they meant to leave all their memories behind? Misty had a vague idea of Redbridge, it was where her grandparents had lived, and they used to go and visit almost every weekend when Misty was small.

'It's right by Pop's old place,' Dad continued as if reading her thoughts. 'You remember, don't you? You used to love it there.'

Misty couldn't deny that she had adored visiting the home that her father had grown up in, hearing all the old stories from when he was young, but it didn't mean she wanted to live there. It was an old council estate and Misty had always been secretly proud of her father for leaving it behind, even if she had never mentioned it to him before.

'I liked *visiting*,' she answered spitefully. 'When I knew we were able to leave at the end of the day and come back here, to *our* home.'

Her dad looked at her with a mixture of sadness and shame that passed briefly over his face and made Misty turn her back and run up to her room, slamming the door loudly behind her for good measure. The reverberations made everything in her bedroom shake and a small china doll that her mum had given her fell and smashed into pieces on the wooden floor below. Misty sank down heavily onto the bed and started to cry. It felt like a bad omen. Misty knew one thing for certain, she wasn't leaving this house and her mother's memory behind.

The following morning, Misty was up in her bedroom when she heard the sharp honking of a car horn outside. She hadn't left her room since the previous evening and as she raced downstairs to find out who it was, she bumped straight into her dad who was already waiting in the hallway by the front door.

'Put your shoes on. We're going out,' he announced.

Misty was about to open her mouth to protest that she already had plans with her friends, but she took one look at her dad's resolute expression and knew it would be pointless. She thrust her feet into her furry winter boots, grabbing her coat as her father hustled her out of the door.

'Morning.' Dave greeted them cheerfully. 'Are you ready to go?'

Misty didn't know if she was ready or not, so she kept her mouth shut and slid soundlessly into the back, as her dad took the passenger seat.

'Let's go!' Dave turned onto the road and rows of houses passed by in a blur.

Misty had managed to zone out completely and wasn't paying even the slightest bit of attention to her surroundings when they came to a sudden halt around twenty minutes later. They must have only been a short distance from home, but the houses couldn't have been more different. The smart red-brick semis had been replaced with rundown pebbledash terraces.

'Here we are,' Dave announced with the optimism of a gameshow host.

'Where are we?' Misty asked, her curiosity finally getting the better of her now that they were out of the car.

'This is Dave's parents' old place, the one I was telling you about last night,' her dad answered. 'Shall we take a look inside?'

''I'll just stay out here if that's ok?' Misty kicked a stray stone down the street in front of her.

'Suit yourself,' her dad replied as he made his way over to the house, Dave following close behind. About ten minutes later they reappeared, and her dad was shaking Dave's hand and smiling happily, a look of relief on his face.

'It's a great house,' Dad told her as they climbed back into the car. 'Are you sure you don't want to take a look around?'

Misty nodded, her eyes still glued to the pavement. 'I'm sure.'

She couldn't help feeling angry that her dad had brought her here unannounced. *What was the point of looking at this house if we don't have to move in the end?* Her dad looked like he was about to say something but at the last minute he seemed to decide against it. His mouth settled into an unwavering line, and he nodded at Dave, signalling that they were ready to leave.

'I'm really grateful, Dave,' he said quietly. 'It's perfect. Exactly what we need.'

'No problem. Anything I can do to help.'

Dave switched on the radio, and they passed the rest of the journey home without speaking. Misty looked glumly out of the window at the unknown streets and felt relieved when they finally turned a corner and were in familiar territory once more.

Later that evening, when her dad tried once again to raise the subject of moving, Misty refused to be drawn into the conversation.

'I've got a school project to do,' she told him at dinner. 'I don't have time to talk about this right now.'

'OK,' her dad said, backing down immediately. He always commented on his daughter's stubbornness and if he pushed her, Misty would only push back even harder. 'Well, let me know when you do want to talk.'

Misty was picked up bright and early the next morning. It was Jasmine's fourteenth birthday, and the three girls were going to an adventure park for a day of outdoor activities. As she was still trying to avoid speaking to her dad and felt guilty asking for money, she had taken the thirty-pound entrance fee out of the savings account her mum had opened for her when she was a baby. She wasn't meant to touch the money until she was eighteen and she knew her dad would be disappointed if he ever found out what she had spent it on.

When the girls arrived at the woodland, they were each given a helmet and a map which showed them the route through a treetop assault course. Misty gulped nervously, she wasn't a huge fan of heights and the idea of swinging through the trees on flimsy rope bridges wasn't really her idea of fun, even if they would be clipped on.

'This is going to be so good,' Ruby exclaimed enthusiastically, always up for a new challenge.

As the girls made their way round the course, with Jasmine's mum keeping a watchful eye on them from below, Misty couldn't help feeling slightly annoyed as her two friends laughed and joked around as she struggled to move through the high branches, her legs trembling beneath her as she went. By the time they got to the end of the course, Misty was bubbling with a barely contained anger.

'That was amazing,' Jasmine said contentedly. 'Thanks for coming.'

'You're being very quiet today,' Ruby remarked when Misty didn't say anything. 'Is everything ok?'

'Fine,' Misty replied abruptly. 'Why do you keep asking me that?'

'What do you mean?' Ruby asked. 'I was only checking if you were feeling all right.'

'You have been acting a bit strangely the last couple of weeks,' Jasmine added. 'We're just worried about you, that's all.'

'There's nothing to worry about. You know I don't like heights.'

Jasmine's face went pink, and she looked as if she was about to cry. 'I'm sorry I brought you here,' she said as she turned and stalked off towards her mother who was waiting for them near the entrance.

'Now look what you've done,' Ruby snapped. 'You know how sensitive she can be. Why are you being like this?'

As Ruby ran off to join the others, Misty felt as though she was being slowly engulfed by all of her secrets, a monster of her own making, and she felt powerless to stop it. She couldn't admit that she was worried, that she couldn't really afford the entrance fee for the park today, that she was still feeling furious with her dad and frightened that they were going to have to move. So instead of saying any of these things she had turned her resentment onto her friends and managed to ruin her best friend's birthday as a result. And now she had guilt and shame to add to the heady cocktail of emotions that were swirling around inside her, tossing and turning anxiously, unable to find a release.

Misty was relieved when she was finally dropped off at home. If Jasmine's mum, Ivy, had noticed the tense silence in the car on the drive back into town, she hadn't commented on it. Perhaps she thought the girls were exhausted from a day of hard physical exertion and fresh country air. When they arrived outside her house, Misty slammed the car door behind her and ran inside without looking back.

'Misty is that you?' her dad called from the living room. 'Don't you think we should sit down and talk about what happened yesterday?'

Misty's shoulders slumped in defeat; she was way too tired to protest. She sat down on the sofa next to him, burying her face in her hands. All she wanted to do was to go up to her room and forget everything; her friends, the adventure park and, most of all, the idea of moving.

'What did you think of the house?' Dad ventured hesitantly. 'I know you didn't see that much of it.'

'I know you don't want to move,' he continued when she didn't reply. 'But we might not be able to afford to stay here much longer. The rent's too expensive and Dave's offered us a very cheap deal on his place. Will you at least give it a chance?'

'I'm not going,' Misty replied. '*You* said we probably wouldn't have to move. You said everything would be fine.'

'I thought if I found a new job straightaway, nothing would have to change.'

'You lied to me,' Misty said accusingly, her feelings springing out from where they had been gathering deep within her. 'You promised me, after Mum got sick, that you would never keep anything from me again. That you would always tell me the truth, however hard it was. We're meant to be a team, remember? We're meant to be on the same side.'

'I know and I'm sorry, I thought I was protecting you. I didn't mean to lie to you.' Her dad's head was hanging dolefully from his shoulders as if he wished he could hide from her, and his voice shook as he continued. 'I've tried my best to look after you these past few years. I never wanted any of this to happen. But the fact remains that if I don't find a job soon, we're going to have to leave this house.'

'How soon?' Misty asked, her voice softening slightly at her dad's anxious tone.

'I've spoken to Dave, and he says we can move in next month. I've given notice to our landlord, just in case.'

'Next month?' Misty exclaimed.

Misty felt the ground lurch beneath her as if the Earth had stopped spinning for a moment and then started up again in the opposite direction. She couldn't believe they would have to move so soon. But she also knew that her dad had been doing everything in his power to find a new job and that whatever the future had in store for them both, they had to face it together.

CHAPTER FIVE

By the end of their first week back at school, Misty still hadn't apologised for ruining Jasmine's birthday. It was the longest she had ever gone without speaking to either of her friends and she felt completely wretched without them. To make matters worse, when she got home on Friday afternoon, she found the living room covered in boxes. Her father stood amidst the mountain of cardboard, a look of determined concentration on his face as he threw into them piles of books and photograph albums that had lain untouched since Misty's mother's death.

'What's going on?' Misty tried to make sense of the chaos. Surely, her dad wasn't packing already. It was as if he had already decided they were leaving, that he had given up hope of them being able to stay. Misty's fingers lay frozen on the handle of the door, as though if she went back out and opened it again an altogether different scenario would be waiting for her on the other side.

Her black school bag dangled from the crook of her other arm, a forgotten remnant from earlier that day.

Misty's dad seemed not to have heard her come into the house at all; he seemed solely focused on moving each item from the built-in shelving into a box as quickly as possible, like an ill-fitting game of Jenga.

'Dad?' Misty shouted. 'Dad, what are you doing?'

Misty's dad blinked and shook his head. 'Packing,' he replied tersely as he continued to fill boxes.

'Yes, I can see that. But why?'

Misty wondered briefly if he had sold all of their possessions to make some extra cash, but she didn't really believe that anyone would want their old family photos or the battered paperback books they had bought from car-boot sales and the charity shop on the high street in town.

'We have to go,' he answered. 'Landlord's decided we have to be out by Monday.'

'*What?*'

'You heard me. He's found new tenants already.'

Misty felt her heart lurch, drop down and land somewhere on the floor beneath her feet.

'But we can't move yet,' Misty whispered. 'I thought you said we had another month—'

'That's what I was told.' Her dad stopped packing, his head paused over a half-filled box of CDs. 'I've tried my best. I've tried everything, I really have, but time's up I'm afraid.

At least we're not going to be out on the streets, Dave's happy for us to move to his parents' old place anytime.'

Misty felt her world stand still. Even as she tried to make sense of it all, her dad continued to pack their belongings into boxes. She wished he would stop for a minute and talk to her properly.

'I can't believe this is really happening.'

Suddenly all the frantic activity left her father, his face crumpling up as he visibly deflated, and he rubbed his eyes wearily.

'I don't want to go either,' he said. 'But we don't have any other option. And it's not all bad, we'll be nearer the sea for a start.'

Misty loved the sea; it was one of her favourite things about the city. But she also loved their home. It held so many memories of her mother. Letting go of the house would be like saying goodbye all over again and this time it would be final.

'What about school?' Misty asked.

'You can take the bus. You won't even have to change schools.'

How am I going to keep this *from my friends?* It had been hard enough trying to keep her dad's lost job a secret for six weeks. She was never going to admit that they were living on an estate. She shuddered to think what Ruby would say if she found out. Her best friend had a very particular way of looking at the world and that was putting it politely. Perhaps it was for the best that neither Ruby nor Jasmine seemed to be talking to her at the moment.

She wondered briefly if she should refuse to go but what else could she do? Perhaps it would only be temporary, until her dad found another job. Maybe they could get the house back then. She didn't know how she would fit in on an estate, whether she'd be able to make any friends there.

'Oh, I almost forgot to mention,' Dad said brightly. 'Remember the horses?'

'Horses?'

'Yes, that live on the estate. A whole herd of them. I would have shown you when we went over there, but you were too busy sulking. You probably don't remember but you used to love visiting them with your gran.'

Misty had a vague recollection of petting horses with Granny as a child but she had absolutely zero interest in horses now. She thought they were at best a bit smelly, at worst frightening, all massive hooves and vice-like teeth. *What on earth are horses doing in Redbridge?* But her dad seemed so hopeful that she didn't want to upset him.

'Great,' she replied, doing her best to sound enthusiastic. 'It sounds great.'

Even to her ears this didn't ring true, but her dad was so busy worrying about the future and trying to organise the cluttered sitting room that he seemed to take her words at face value.

'Of course, it'll be a huge adjustment for us both but I'm sure we'll be very happy there. I loved it when I was a boy,' he said, putting a brave face on things. 'We'll still have a whole house and a yard; it really won't be that different at all.'

Misty wondered what a yard was. *Was it the same as a garden?* She thought about the beautiful rose bushes her mother had planted that bloomed in the spring each year. The lush green lawn with the gable-roofed shed at the bottom of it. A yard sounded like more grey to her.

By Saturday morning, the last of the boxes were packed and it was time to say goodbye to the house. A white van was parked outside and Dave began to load all of their worldly possessions into it. Misty had felt queasy all evening, a mixture of nerves about the impending move and sadness about leaving their home behind. She had somehow managed to sort out her own room, refusing to let her dad help as she picked her way through the messy piles that made up the last thirteen years of her life, and mechanically threw it all into boxes as if it had little meaning whatsoever.

Once the van was ready, they stood staring up at the house as if they were strangers. Misty let herself wonder for a moment who would be moving into their home.

Would a new family be as happy as they had been there before her mother had died? Was it possible that their past happiness could have absorbed into the walls, waiting to be released for its new occupants? Misty could imagine a mum, a dad, two children and maybe a dog – the perfect family. She tried to swallow the wave of resentment that rose in her throat when she thought about another family living in their house.

Mum was gone and now so was their home and all the memories that were tied up within it. Misty took one last look at the second-floor window on the lefthand side that had been her bedroom and slowly turned away. She felt as though she was trudging through thick, soupy mud as she forcibly made her way down the front path for the last time and closed the gate behind her with a deafening clang. Dad was waiting for her on the pavement, Dave already behind the wheel of the van ready to leave.

'A new chapter,' Misty's dad said optimistically as he wrapped his right arm tightly round her shoulders.

Misty didn't say anything as they got into their car and started to follow Dave down the street. She could see the house getting smaller in the rearview mirror until they took a left onto the main road, and it suddenly vanished from view. Her eyes felt hot and damp, tears threatening to escape if she let them. She tried to distract herself as they turned left again, and the streets became less familiar, more rundown with last night's beer cans and discarded carrier bags strewn across the pavements. She was surprised to see that amidst the chaos of it all, people were cheerfully going about their morning tasks, smiling and nodding to one another as they passed. *How can they be so happy living here?* she thought.

'We'll be there soon,' Dad shouted over the noise of the engine. 'It's not far now.'

As the shops and pubs fell away behind them, they entered the winding streets of the *cul de sacs* that marked the boundary of the Redbridge Estate. As the car rose swiftly up another hill, Misty noticed a street lined with, what seemed like to her, drab pebbledash houses on either side, before a wide expanse of scrubland opened in front of them. It stretched across the horizon, and, in the distance, you could see the old industrial chimneys that marked the edge of the wasteland. The grass wasn't lush and green like their old back garden; the uneven ground was covered in dirt, and it seemed to Misty that the yellowing grass was struggling to cling on to this treacherous hillside.

As Dad steered the car round so they were driving parallel to the common, Misty saw a glimpse of the horses for the first time. Coloured blotches of red, brown and gold slowly came into focus to reveal four-legged creatures of various shapes and sizes. Some were tethered to the unforgiving ground with old, tattered ropes whilst others roamed freely. Just as quickly as they had appeared, the car turned another corner and the horses vanished from sight as if they had never existed. After driving down a street of four-storey blocks of flats, they pulled up outside a small row of terraces.

'Here we are,' said Dad. 'Welcome to our new home.'

CHAPTER SIX

Although it was still winter, Misty was woken by the stark grey morning light streaming in through the curtainless windows of her new bedroom. Lifeless, empty walls stared listlessly down on her. For a moment she couldn't remember why she was waking up in a bare room full of boxes. Bit by bit the memories of the past week came flooding back as though the boxes were collapsing and revealing the forgotten contents of her mind.

Misty sighed and covered her face with her old duvet, which still smelled comfortingly familiar, like their old house – the fusty, damp odour that seemed to permeate this one hadn't managed to seep into it yet. She was sure if she touched the boxes nearest the window, they would feel cold and wet. It was disgusting. *Were they really meant to live here?*

The previous evening as they'd sat down to dinner, her father had tried to put a positive spin on their new home, but the place was, in Misty's opinion, not just in need of a complete facelift but total demolition. A sharp tweeting sound, followed by a persistent buzz pulled Misty from her thoughts. Her phone was lying on the floor beside her bed, plugged into the wall (which was probably a safety hazard).

It was a message from Ruby asking if Misty wanted to meet her and Jasmine in town. Misty groaned and rolled away from the offending object. She didn't know what to say. She knew that Ruby would be annoyed if she didn't reply straightaway, especially after the incident at the adventure park, but she wasn't ready to face either of them yet.

Another message appeared, this time in the group chat she shared with both of her friends. It was a picture of Jasmine drinking a hot chocolate whilst modelling a pair of flamboyant sparkly purple sunglasses. Misty smiled wistfully; it looked like they were having a great time without her. She felt a sharp pang of resentment just below her heart.

Ping! A picture of the two girls wearing tartan pyjamas, Ruby's were red of course and Jasmine's green and black. Misty had an identical blue set; the girls had been given them as Christmas presents the previous year and they still just about fit into them. She could remember how excited they had all been to receive a matching set. She looked at the message:

Spontaneous sleepover Saturday! Wish you were here! x

At least they seemed to have decided to forgive her. Misty switched the phone on to silent and buried it firmly beneath her pillow. She'd just have to come up with a convincing excuse tomorrow. Pretend she had misplaced her charger or lost her phone or something. For now, she had more pressing things to worry about like trying to tidy this room. If they were going to have to stay here, she might as well make it a bit more homely.

As Misty started unpacking boxes and ferreting out her most prized possessions, there was a knock at her bedroom door. Without waiting for permission, her dad's head appeared, followed by a cup of tea and a plate containing two crumpets.

'Breakfast?' he asked as he nudged open the door.

Misty hadn't thought she was hungry, but the sight of the hot, buttery crumpets made her mouth water.

When she didn't reply, he continued: 'It looks better in here already.'

He gestured to the posters of pop stars that adorned the wall above Misty's bed, and her mother's glass cabinet by the window that was lined with trinkets she had gathered from the shops with Ruby and Jasmine. Looking at it reminded Misty of how much she missed her mum, and now her friends too. As she tried to distract herself, she looked towards the window and caught a glimpse of the horses they had seen the previous day on the common below.

'I need... curtains,' she stuttered, trying not to let her feelings rise to the surface and upset her dad. She needed to prove to him that she could make the best out of their current predicament and not make him feel worse than he already did.

Dad continued as if he hadn't heard her. 'You shouldn't stay cooped up in here all day. Why don't you go out for a walk, get some fresh air? You might make some new friends.'

Misty shuddered. That was the last thing she wanted. They would only be here for a short while, until her dad found a new job, so what was the point?

'Maybe later,' she answered, relenting ever so slightly when she remembered the silent promise she had just made to herself. 'I'm going to finish unpacking first.'

For a moment, Misty's dad looked as though he was going to push the matter, but he just said, 'Ok, well, I'll leave you to it then. I'll be downstairs if you need anything.'

'Thanks, Dad.'

After he left, Misty closed the door and sat down on the unmade bed. *Perhaps Dad has a point*, she thought. *What am I going to do all day?* For the second time that morning, her eyes were drawn to the window and to the barren field in the near distance. A sudden flash of movement caught her eye, but she was determined to ignore it. It would only be one of the horses and of what interest could they possibly be to her?

Despite her best efforts, by eleven o'clock, Misty was extremely bored. Although she was trying not to admit, even to herself, that she had any interest whatsoever in what was happening outside, she couldn't help taking the occasional peek as she started taking books and placing them on the shelf next to her bed.

Across the street, a tiny raven-haired girl and the biggest man Misty had ever seen were, as far as Misty could tell, chasing a stocky black and white horse up and down the side of the field at the end of the road. The horse, who was almost as wide as the man she presumed was its owner, was refusing to be caught. Misty couldn't help but laugh at the look of sheer purpose on the small girl's face as she tried to lunge for the rope that was dancing around the large cob's feet. The even larger man had given up pursuing him and was panting, red-faced, with his hands gripping his knees.

She was about to go back to arranging her books, when the little girl looked straight up at the window and Misty quickly ducked out of sight. She wondered if she had been seen. She didn't have to wonder for very long, however, as there was a sudden, loud *tap* on the pane of glass next to her. She looked down and saw that there was now another girl, about her own age, standing directly across the street, who was gesturing to her to come downstairs. There was no use trying to hide.

As Misty tried to decide what to do, the older girl shouted, 'Posh people in Redbridge, who'd have thought it,' which made the younger girl giggle uncontrollably. The older girl had somehow managed to catch the big cow-coloured horse and was holding onto him by the side of his headcollar with a smug smirk on her face. 'She probably thinks she's too good for us,' she continued.

'I don't,' Misty muttered to herself. She tried to keep placing her books on the shelves, arranging them methodically by author and series but she couldn't stop thinking about what the girl had said. How was she supposed to fit in here if they had already made up their minds about her? That she was too posh for Redbridge. It was a good job she'd be leaving soon. That this was only temporary. She'd just have to avoid those girls until then.

By mid-afternoon, Misty had finished most of her unpacking and when she glanced out at the sky once more, she saw that it had turned an even darker, more threatening shade of grey. It wasn't exactly great weather for a walk, but with nothing else to do, curiosity got to the better of her and she grabbed a waterproof jacket and decided to head outside.

'I'll be back later,' she called to her dad as she opened the door and peered nervously out into the street. There was no sign of the earlier commotion, but she felt very exposed as invisible droplets of rain drifted down aimlessly and landed on the tip of her nose. Misty pulled up her hood as she began to walk, head down, in the opposite direction of the common. She didn't want to risk bumping into the stone-throwing girl or her mini companion any time soon.

Misty pushed on through the dull drizzle and up through the windy streets of the estate, a sense of sheer desolation coming over her. All the houses that she passed looked identical and with no destination in mind she began to wonder why she had bothered to leave the house at all. It was starting to get dark, and she worried that she might get lost and unknowingly end up somewhere she shouldn't be. Just as panic began to set in, the high street that they had driven down the previous day came into view. Her shoulders relaxed, and she let out a small, anxious exhale as the lights of the shops came into focus through the blurry rain.

As she turned onto the safety of the well-lit high street, Misty heard the unmistakeable clopping of hooves behind her and ducked quickly round the corner of a nearby house so she could hide herself from view. When she finally plucked up the courage to peer out of her hiding place, she saw the figure of a small grey horse carrying a boy of a similar age to her own on its back. It seemed you couldn't escape from the horses; they were everywhere. She was glad she hadn't been seen, but it had been a close call and she wished she was back inside the confines of their new house. It was better than being out on the street where anything could happen to her.

She continued to watch as the boy and the grey horse rode past, turned right onto the high street and disappeared from sight. She heard the sound of a car beeping its horn urgently. *Fancy riding a horse down a main street like that,* Misty thought. *What if they got into an accident?* Misty shuddered; she couldn't imagine why anyone would do something so stupid. One thing was certain, she needed to stay as far away from the horses and their owners as possible. First stone-throwing and now this, she didn't want to have anything to do with such reckless behaviour. Though she had to admit that a small part of her was curious about what it would feel like to have the freedom to go wherever you pleased in this way, seemingly unconstrained by everyday conventions.

As abruptly as this thought appeared in her mind, she shook her head fiercely as if to dislodge it. Once she was sure that the boy and the horse weren't coming back her way, she left her concealed spot and began walking quickly in the opposite direction towards home.

CHAPTER SEVEN

The next morning, much to her relief, Misty managed to walk to the bus stop without bumping into anyone untoward. The route to the bus stop went past the common. In the cold, clear morning light Misty watched as some of the horses methodically cut through the patchy grass with their massive teeth while others stood, knee deep in winter mud, as if waiting for someone to come and rescue them. It was quite a sight, these horses stranded on the city hillside, and Misty felt suddenly drawn to them, but then she remembered what the older girl had said and hurried ahead in case she might be nearby, waiting to jump out and startle her.

She located the bus stop easily; it was the only shelter on a windy stretch of road that fell away to scrubland on her right and overlooked more identikit pebbledash houses on the left. There were a couple of elderly people waiting when she arrived who muttered 'hello' but otherwise ignored her. No one in school uniform. By the time the bus came five minutes later, she was already numb with cold and couldn't wait to find a seat to burrow down into for the rest of the journey.

The bus rumbled rambunctiously down the shabby streets Misty had seen from the car window on Saturday morning. This time, as if in reverse, the streets became wider the closer they got to Misty's old neighbourhood. The buildings became more familiar, and Misty realised they were almost at her school. She would need to get off a stop early if she didn't want anyone to see her coming in on the bus from Redbridge. She pressed the bell and sprang to her feet, hastily grabbing her school bag and swaying precariously towards the door as the bus continued to move. It suddenly screeched to a halt with a loud sighing noise as if letting out a long-held breath and spat Misty out of its doors and onto the street.

The low-lying sun blinded her for a moment. As she squinted through the dazzling brightness, Misty could see that she was about a ten-minute walk from her school. She looked round to check that no one had spotted her and headed off rapidly. At last, she could see the imposing black gates up ahead and as she rushed through them she paused to check her phone; it was 8.45, she was just in time.

Ruby and Jasmine were waiting in their usual spot on the other side of the playground. Misty took a deep breath, fixed her best 'everything is fine' smile in place and strolled over to meet them. Before Misty even reached them, Ruby launched into her interrogation.

'How was your weekend? We were worried when we didn't hear *anything* from you. We thought something might have happened to you.' For all her bossy exterior, Ruby always knew when something was up with one of her friends. She would make a great detective some day.

'Sorry,' Misty mumbled. 'I was just really busy helping my dad... and then I misplaced my phone... and I thought I had lost it but then—'

'You really should have let us know you were ok,' Ruby interrupted.

'I know,' Misty conceded, focusing her eyes on the ground, trying to summon up the courage to find the words she needed to say. 'And I'm really sorry for how I acted on your birthday, Jasmine. It was totally out of order.'

'It's fine,' Jasmine replied, awkwardly shuffling from one foot to the other. 'I should have remembered how much you dislike heights.'

'It was selfish of me,' Misty continued. 'It was meant to be your special day not mine.'

'Don't worry, I forgive you,' Jasmine said, clearly trying to avoid confrontation. 'We're going to have another sleepover at mine next weekend. You will come, won't you?'

'I'll have to check with my dad, but it should be ok.'

Misty couldn't think of a convincing excuse not to go to the sleepover, and she wanted to show her friends how sorry she really was. It was at Jasmine's, so there would be no need to mention Redbridge at all.

'Great,' Ruby replied. 'I'm glad that's sorted. I can't wait for us all to be together this weekend.'

To Misty's ears, Ruby words felt a bit loaded, but she was probably imagining things, she was so on edge about everything that was happening at home. Misty had to go to the sleepover now, though; if she didn't, they'd know that something still wasn't right and start asking even more probing questions. She couldn't keep avoiding her friends and coming up with weird excuses for her strange behaviour for ever.

'Yeah, that'll be great,' she said. 'Roll on Friday.'

When Misty got home from school that evening, the surfaces of the small galley kitchen were lined with unusual items of food. It wasn't the food itself that was remarkable, tins of beans and cans of soup, value porridge oats and jumbo bags of pasta, it just wasn't anything that they would normally have bought.

'Where's all this come from?' she asked her dad who was sitting at a small wooden table beside the back door. Their old six-seater dining table wouldn't have fit inside this small, terraced house, so it was packed away in storage with the rest of their things.

'Judy dropped it round earlier.'

'Who's Judy? And how come she's doing our shopping for us now? Is it all part of the Redbridge service?' Misty giggled.

'You could say that,' Dad replied firmly, as if he didn't want to discuss the matter any further. 'Anyway, we got talking, turns out she has a daughter about the same age as you. They might pop by later to say hello.'

Misty took another look at the bags of shopping on the worktop, slightly taken aback by her dad's abrupt tone. Lying next to them, partially hidden under a can of soup, was a leaflet. The word *foodbank* leaped out from its cover in bold green lettering. She didn't understand. *Surely, we can't be that desperate?* Misty had a vague idea of what a foodbank was and thought it was for people who were completely destitute, who didn't have any money at all, and couldn't even afford to pay their own bills.

'Dad? It says this food is from the local foodbank. But that can't be right, can it?'

When her dad didn't answer she knew that it was true. They really *were* those people now. The people Misty had always secretly looked down on, that she'd assumed were too lazy to work or caught up in some kind of criminal activity. It looked like they were going to have to live on baked beans, plain pasta and tomato soup for the rest of the week. And Misty didn't even like tomato soup.

'It's just for the time being,' Dad said, his voice breaking into her thoughts. 'I'm sure I'll hear back from one of those jobs I applied for soon.'

Misty tried to ignore the sinking feeling in the pit of her stomach and to smile reassuringly and pretend that nothing was wrong. She couldn't tell anyone at school about this. What would Ruby and Jasmine say if they found out?

Later that evening, as promised, Judy appeared with her oldest daughter, Carin, in tow. When she heard the firm, business-like rap on the door, Misty's heart sank, she had been hoping they wouldn't be able to make it. *I don't want to be introduced to anyone*, she thought stubbornly, least of all to people her own age, who would probably just make fun of her like the girl who had been throwing stones at her window. But before she could go upstairs to hide in her room, her dad had answered the door and Judy bustled into the room.

'You must be Misty,' Judy beamed. She had a smile that could light up a whole town and Misty could see why her dad, who was usually quite reserved when it came to meeting new people, had warmed to her instantly. 'And this is Carin.'

Misty's jaw dropped as Judy gestured towards the tall, birdlike girl who until now had been hiding behind her. Although she had her gaze lowered meekly towards the floor, standing with her mother in their front room, Misty was sure that the girl stood in front of her was none another than the stone-thrower.

'Why don't you two go on upstairs?' Misty's dad said encouragingly. 'You can show Carin your new bedroom. You don't want us adults cramping your style.'

Misty gave her dad a treacherous glare, before turning around and thundering up the stairs not even waiting to see if Carin was following behind her.

'Go on,' she heard Judy call gently from below. 'I'm sure she won't bite.'

Maybe I will. Misty's dark mood persisted as she waited for Carin to catch up. Away from the adults, the other girl's bashfulness was replaced with a confident, boisterous air. She still looked like she'd rather not be there but now she seemed bored rather than shy. Misty fixed her gaze on the wall above her bed, determined not to be the one to break the awkward silence that had settled over the room.

'Nice room,' Carin offered eventually, kicking the back of her heels off Misty's bedframe noisily, her shoes still on, as she took in the posters and books lining the walls. 'Got any brothers and sisters?'

'No,' Misty answered.

'I've got two,' Carin continued undeterred by Misty's lack of interest. 'An older brother and a younger sister. Total nightmare.' She chuckled to herself. 'You're lucky, having the whole place to yourself.'

'Doesn't feel like it,' Misty mumbled despite her best efforts to keep quiet.

'You're not annoyed about the stone-throwing, are you?' Carin asked. 'I wanted to say hello. Introduce myself.'

'Funny way of showing it,' Misty objected.

'I was just trying to get your attention, so you'd come outside,' she explained. 'I didn't realise you required an *official invitation.*'

'You said I was posh,' Misty replied defensively. 'I'm not *posh*. My dad grew up here you know.'

'Ok! Ok! Fine.' Carin held up her hands in mock surrender. 'You just seem a bit uptight is all.'

You'd be uptight if you'd had to move here at a moment's notice and leave all your friends behind, Misty thought sadly. She paused as she struggled to put her thoughts into words.

'It's just different here,' she tried to explain. 'From what I'm used to.'

'Well, I'll bring the red carpet round next time, shall I?' Carin laughed, before changing tack when she saw the look on Misty's face. 'Relax, I'm only joking. Look, I need to go, but why don't you come down and see the horses after you finish school tomorrow? I'll introduce you to everyone.'

'Fine,' Misty stammered reluctantly, thinking back to what she had witnessed only the previous day. 'I mean... I'll think about it.'

'Don't think too hard.' Carin was in a full-blown fit of giggles now, her earlier boredom forgotten. 'You might pop.'

In response, Misty screwed up her face and glowered at Carin as she slowly backed out of the room, her hands held in front of her chest as if in retreat from the enemy.

'See you tomorrow!' she called out chirpily behind her.

Misty could hear the muffled thud of footsteps on carpet as Carin raced down the stairs. She heard Carin call out 'goodbye' to her dad before the latch clicked and the door slammed loudly behind her. You could hear everything in this tiny house and from what Misty had witnessed so far, Carin didn't seem able to do anything quietly.

'See that wasn't so bad, was it?' Dad asked when Misty came back downstairs.

'If you say so.' Misty raised her eyebrows and looked round at the now-empty sitting room. 'You and Judy seem to be getting on pretty well.'

She tried to quell the weight of sadness that settled in her chest when she thought of her dad moving forward with his life. *Doesn't he deserve to be happy?* But as hard as she tried, she couldn't imagine that one day it would no longer be just the two of them.

'She certainly is a nice woman,' he agreed, before adding, as if reading her thoughts, 'but don't worry, you won't be getting a stepmother any time soon.'

'Thank goodness for that,' Misty joked uneasily, unsure of what she should say or do next.

'How did you and Carin get on?'

'Ok,' Misty said, glad of the swift change of subject. 'She's invited me to go and meet some of the other kids and see the horses tomorrow.'

'That's great,' her dad replied, seemingly reassured, already pottering around distractedly as he tidied the living room. 'You should definitely go along.'

'Maybe,' Misty answered noncommittally. She still wasn't quite sure what to make of Carin or the boy she had seen on horseback yesterday. 'I'll see how I feel.'

Her dad picked up the two empty mugs that were nestled closely beside one another on the coffee table and Misty yawned, the busy day suddenly catching up with her. She climbed the stairs with heavy feet, and as her head hit the pillow, her mind continued whirling with all the changes and surprises of the last few days. Eventually she fell into a restless night's sleep.

CHAPTER EIGHT

When the alarm on her phone woke Misty for school the next day, for one peaceful moment she thought she was back at their old house; it was only when she opened her eyes to the dismal view of her new bedroom that she remembered. Not only that they had moved and her dad had lost his job, but that there was also an aggressive girl, who she now knew as Carin, who threw stones against windows and kicked her heels against bedframes, and a lady named Judy who dropped round groceries from the local foodbank.

It was all too much to take in. Misty groaned, rolled over and tried to go back to sleep. She couldn't face school today; Ruby's suspicious glances and accusatory state-ments; trying to act as if everything was normal when it was as far from normal as it possibly could be. Jasmine's worried glances and furtive peacekeeping. There was no way she was going. She knew she wouldn't be able to get back to sleep with all these thoughts churning round like a washing machine inside her head, but that didn't mean she had to go anywhere.

She hadn't heard any movement on the landing outside her bedroom door, so she assumed her dad was still asleep. Even though it had only been a few days since they had moved in, Misty had noticed that her dad was spending more and more time in his room. His optimism seemed to be starting to fade, and Misty couldn't get used to him being at home all the time when he had previously been so busy with work. If she stayed quiet, when he finally appeared, he would assume she had already left for school. She pulled the duvet over her head and tried to decide what to do next. She knew she couldn't stay holed up in her bedroom all day; she'd starve for one thing and be bored out of her brains for another.

Misty decided that she would have to leave the house, but that didn't mean she was going to school. She would email her form tutor from her dad's account (he used the same password for everything and had asked Misty to memorise it in case of emergency) and find somewhere else to go. She didn't know where but there were sure to be plenty of hiding places scattered around the estate. She also wanted to avoid Carin, but she should be at school by now anyway. She had noticed the Redbridge secondary school when she was out walking on Sunday, an imposingly large building that looked at least twice the size of Misty's school.

She dressed in an old pair of jeans and a sweater, brushed her tangled red hair and opened her bedroom door, grimacing as the hinges creaked menacingly. She paused for a moment, holding her breath, but the door to her dad's room stayed firmly shut. There was no sound apart from the gentle drip of the bathroom tap which refused to stop however hard you turned it. Misty crept across the landing and down the stairs into the living room below.

In the bags on the kitchen counter, she found a box of cereal bars and grabbed a couple on her way out of the back door. The latch clicked but there was still no sign of movement upstairs. A small grey yard, which was just large enough to house the bins, led out onto a narrow alleyway lined on either side with more identical terraced houses, a mirror image of their own. There was a small breezeblock shed, the remnants of an outside toilet, by the back gate but Misty didn't much fancy staying in there all day.

As she was attempting to come up with a plan, she heard the rhythmic clatter of hooves on concrete and saw the splotchy cow-like horse she had seen the day before careening towards her. For a split second, Misty wondered if the horse had escaped again but as it came nearer, she noticed the leather headpiece and reins that ran down its back and the smart black-and-red painted cart attached to them.

At the end of the reins there was a boy who looked to be a couple of years older than Misty. His light-brown hair stuck up at surprising right angles from the centre of his head and his pale freckled skin and green eyes gave him the look of a time-travelling urchin from long ago. As he got closer, he gave a roguish smile and pulled hard at the reins which made the horse lift its head in protest and stop just in front of her.

'Why aren't you at school?' Misty asked accusingly, annoyed at having been discovered so easily.

'Why aren't *you* at school?' the boy countered, his grin spreading upwards towards his sticky-out ears.

Misty wasn't sure how to respond, the real reason was far too complicated to explain, and she wasn't about to admit that she was too ashamed to face her best friends to this scruffy stranger.

Instead, she asked, 'And whose horse is that?'

'How do you know he isn't mine?'

'I don't, I don't know *who* he belongs to. That's why I'm asking you.'

'This is Colin. Colin the cob. He's Fred's horse, isn't he? I'm just taking him for a bit of a ride. A joyride.'

The boy laughed as if he found his own joke hysterical. Misty frowned.

'Does Fred know you've stolen his horse?'

'Hang on a minute. Who said anything about stealing

him? I'm just borrowing him for the time being, you see? I'm not doing anyone any harm.'

The boy spoke in the persuasive riddles of an adult. It was as if he'd spent hardly any time around children of his own age. He had an almost otherworldly, timeless quality about him, as if he'd just popped up from the pages of a storybook. Misty couldn't help but warm to him a little though she tried her best to conceal it.

'What's your name?' Misty asked, surprised to find that she was actually interested in hearing his response.

'Dylan,' he replied openly. 'What's your name? Are you new round here?'

'I'm Misty,' She hesitated before continuing. 'Sort of, but I'm not staying very long. I'm just... visiting... someone.'

Dylan seemed to take everything Misty said at face value and didn't ask too many questions or call her 'posh'. He had an open, kind way about him and Misty felt instantly she could trust him. Then his facial expression changed unexpectedly as if the wind had caught it and he looked as though he was searching her face for an answer to an unspoken question he hadn't yet thought to ask her. He hesitated, but only for a second, and, making up his mind he asked, 'Do you want to come with me?'

Misty had no idea where Dylan was going but she did need to go somewhere, so against her better judgement, she heard herself agree. It was only once she'd climbed up and was settled beside him on the hard wooden seat that she thought to ask where they were going.

'You'll see,' Dylan replied. The cheeky grin was back again, and Misty had a sinking feeling that she might come to regret her decision to go with him.

It took just over an hour to arrive at the beach but as soon as she saw the sea, Misty realised exactly where Dylan had brought them. Her heart lurched at the sight of the sandy cove surrounded by foreboding rocky cliffs, and the churning grey waves that slapped angrily against the land at this time of year. In the summer, the Merryford beachfront was a calm oasis and Misty had been coming here with both of her parents ever since she was small. Until her mum had passed away and the sea had abruptly disappeared from their lives for good.

'Isn't it magic?' Dylan exclaimed. He was blissfully unaware of the memories that being here brought back to her. 'The sea is totally wild this time of year.'

'It's... lovely,' Misty replied wistfully, unsure of how to steer the conversation back onto safer ground. 'I've always loved the sea.'

'Have you been here before?' Dylan asked curiously.

'No, never,' Misty lied, not wanting to admit how much the coast reminded her of her mother. 'I just meant... generally.'

Dylan had pulled Colin up in front of a row of dilapidated beach huts and jumped down to untangle the large horse from the reins that enclosed him. He gently removed Colin's bridle but left on his headcollar and lead rope.

'On you get,' Dylan said, gesturing towards Colin's bare back.

'What?' Misty spluttered nervously. 'There's absolutely no way I'm getting on that thing.'

'Suit yourself then, you don't know what you're missing.'

Somehow Dylan managed to launch himself through the air and jump up onto Colin's back all in one circus-like move. Misty fought down the urge to clap and gasp in amazement. Before she even had time to react Dylan was away, halfway down the beach, galloping fearlessly across the long stretch of sand.

She watched as Dylan raced back along the wet ground towards her, his grin wider than ever, and crash to a halt just in front of her. She tried not to look too impressed. It was getting chilly, and she didn't want to hang around on the deserted, windswept seashore for too much longer. They'd both get hypothermia.

'It's freezing,' she said, her teeth chattering loudly. 'Do you mind if we go home?'

'Isn't it a bit early to be going home?' Dylan asked sceptically, as if he knew exactly why she was there, on the beach, with him.

Misty tried to swallow the guilty feeling that was nervously crawling up her throat from her stomach. She must have failed to conceal her true emotions as Dylan continued to watch her curiously.

'Don't worry, there's plenty we can do to warm up,' he said agreeably. 'Sure you don't want a ride?'

'No thanks,' Misty replied, though she had started to shake from the cold.

By now, Dylan had dismounted and had tied Colin up to the cart. He reached inside and pulled out a thick wool blanket from beneath the seat.

'Here you go,' he said as he handed it to her. 'Wrap yourself up in this.'

Misty accepted his offering and encased herself like a mummy. The biting wind eased instantly. It was almost lunchtime and her stomach growled loudly, the saltiness of their seaside surroundings making her hunger feel more urgent somehow.

'Got anything to eat?' Dylan asked. 'I'm starving.'

Misty remembered the cereal bars that she had dropped into her bag that morning when she had snuck away from the house. It seemed so long ago, and Redbridge felt a world away from where they were now. As the tide moved in and out in time with her own breathing, Misty felt something that had been tightly wound inside of her start to uncoil. She breathed out all her worries and let them scatter like leaves into the air in front of her. She wasn't in a rush to leave any longer but instead wanted to stay on the beach, watching the now much calmer waves roll tenderly against the shore.

Silently, not wanting to break the peaceful moment, she reached into her bag and handed Dylan one of the breakfast bars. He ripped open the packaging and munched loudly beside her, unaware of her own wish for quiet.

'Not much of a lunch, is it?' Dylan asked. 'Got any money for chips?'

Misty looked round and noticed a winding, shingly path leading up to a small kiosk that seemed to hang precariously from the side of the cliff above them. The hut was painted a muted creamy colour with bright blue lines around the edges and a large sign on the front spelled out FISH AND CHIPS in clear, simple lettering. She didn't remember seeing it there when she was younger, but they had always brought a picnic, so maybe she wouldn't have noticed the solitary shack in the distance.

'I might have a pound somewhere,' Misty said, rooting around in the bottom of her bag. 'Do you think it'll be enough?'

'Should be. Let's go and have a look.'

Dylan rose to his feet and pulled Misty up by her hand. She unfurled herself from the blanket like a Russian doll shedding its extra layers and wobbled unsteadily over the uneven dunes. The sky was starting to turn stormy again, black clouds encroaching on the horizon.

'Do you want my jacket?' Dylan asked as they made their way onto the path.

'I'll be all right,' Misty replied, knowing that the hike up the steep hill would warm her up soon enough. Once they reached the top, she was struggling to catch her breath and paused surreptitiously for a moment, pretending to look through her bag. For some reason she didn't want Dylan to see her in a moment of weakness, to think she wasn't as strong as he was, or as capable.

The small kiosk was dimly lit with overhead strobe lighting. Inside, an older woman stood looking out vacantly over the water, as if she was keeping an eye on the approaching storm. She seemed slightly perplexed by the interruption, as if she wasn't expecting customers any time soon.

'One small chips, please,' Misty ordered tentatively.

'Coming up,' the woman replied briskly as she turned away from the view towards the deep fat frier that was bubbling hot oil behind her.

Once Misty had handed over her pound coin and received a tightly wrapped parcel of chips in return, Dylan took her to a bench that looked out over the water, where they could keep a watchful eye on Colin as they ate.

'Delicious.' Dylan sighed deliberately as he stretched out his full belly. 'You must be feeling much cosier now?'

'Definitely,' Misty agreed. The package in her hands and the chips in her stomach were radiating much needed heat throughout her entire body.

They sat for a while watching the waves before making their way back down to the shoreline, where Colin stood waiting patiently for them to return. When he saw Dylan approaching, he let out a whicker in greeting but made no attempt to move towards them.

'Do you think he's hungry?' Misty asked. She eyed Colin warily, but couldn't help feeling sorry for him, standing alone all that time in the freezing wind.

'I fed him just before we left, so he should be fine until we get back, he's got plenty of reserves don't you worry!' Dylan gestured towards Colin's sturdy, round middle. 'Do you want to see the caves before we head home?'

Misty didn't have the heart to tell Dylan that she had already seen the caves on previous visits to the coast with her parents. She used to spend hours exploring with her dad, searching the rockpools that had been left behind by the tide for the smallest of sea creatures and discarded shells to add to her collection. It would have meant admitting that she had been here before and she didn't want him to think of her as a liar. Despite everything, she was having such a nice time with him, and couldn't spoil it all by admitting the truth just yet. So, she spent the rest of the afternoon following along behind Dylan as he showed her the caves that were hidden on the other side of the rocks that split the beach in two.

Once Dylan had hitched Colin back on to the cart and they were both settled on the wooden seat behind him, they started their journey back towards Redbridge. The country lanes were lined with wide hedges on either side and Misty tensed every time a car approached, hurtling it seemed like a rocket from the other direction, hemming them in. Once the cars had whooshed past, she relaxed back into the seat, soothed by the steady plod of Colin's plate-sized hooves on the tarmac beneath them.

Suddenly, Misty felt a small twinge of guilt as she thought of her phone lying abandoned in the depths of her bag. She realised that she hadn't thought about Ruby and Jasmine for the entire day as she had been so caught up in her seaside adventures with Dylan. She wondered if her friends were missing her at all or if they were getting used to her absence from their lives, like a single shoe lying long forgotten at the bottom of a wardrobe.

All too soon the large hedges were replaced by the now recognisable rows of pebbledash terraces, and Misty tried to push herself down further into the seat so that no one would see her.

'Shall I drop you off where I found you?' Dylan asked, breaking the silence.

Misty took a deep breath, finally summoning up the courage to check her phone. She ignored the stream of message alerts waiting for her and saw that it was nearly three o'clock. She couldn't go home yet. Her dad would probably notice if she turned up an hour earlier than usual.

'No, that's ok,' she replied, pushing away thoughts of her friends. 'Why don't you show me where you keep Colin?'

CHAPTER NINE

Colin's owner, Fred, lived in a static caravan at the edge of the common, which was, to Misty's relief, at the furthest distance from her new house. Across a small concrete yard was a ramshackle set of outbuildings where, Dylan had informed Misty, Colin was stabled. Just as they were about to put Colin away and leave, Fred stumbled out of his caravan, his face bright red with anger.

'I've told you to leave that horse alone,' he shouted, shaking his finger at Dylan. 'He don't belong to you.'

Misty thought they were really in for it, but Dylan didn't look the slightest bit troubled by Fred's furious outburst.

'Just keeping him, and you, on your toes, Uncle Fred,' Dylan smirked. 'After all, you could both do with some exercise.'

'Why you cheeky little—'

'This is Misty, by the way,' Dylan interrupted. 'She's new round here. Staying on the other side of the estate.'

Fred turned his attention to Misty and his face broke into a friendly smile. 'I hope my nephew isn't causing you too much bother.'

'I've been showing her around,' Dylan replied vaguely. 'Showing her the sights.'

'I'll give you sights in a minute,' Fred said, but his voice was gentler now. 'Now get inside. Your mum'll have my guts for garters when she finds out you've been at it again.'

'Why don't you come in and meet my mum?' Dylan asked Misty. 'She might be less annoyed with me if you're there to distract her.'

Misty had been ready to leave but as she still had about an hour to kill, she agreed to go with him. Dylan's house faced the common, and was adjacent to the yard where Fred kept his caravan. From the outside, it looked much the same as her current house, but as soon as Dylan opened the door, she could see that his was, in contrast to hers, almost alive with colour. Rosettes of every shade lined the walls of the living room, alongside what seemed like hundreds of framed photographs of horses of all varieties, and tarnished silver trophies took pride of place on top of the mantelpiece above an ancient-looking gas fire.

'Most of those belong to my sister,' Dylan explained. 'She's the competitive one out of the three of us.'

'The three of you?'

'I'm the eldest, then there's Carin, she's in the middle, and Bethany's the youngest,' Dylan continued as if she already knew he had sisters.

'Carin's your sister?' Misty blurted out in surprise. She had never stopped to think about whether Dylan had any siblings, let alone that he might be related to the only other people she had met on the estate so far. 'So that means—'

Just as Misty was about to slot in the final piece of the puzzle, Judy appeared from the kitchen wearing oven gloves and an apron. She looked slightly flustered as a blast of heat followed closely behind her.

'Hello Misty,' she said, seemingly unperturbed when she saw the pair of them together. 'I see you've met my son. Hope he's not been up to mischief.'

'Hi Judy,' Misty said, stumbling over the words as if she had a set of marbles hidden behind her teeth.

At that moment, the front door crashed open, making the photographs wobble precariously, and Carin entered the house with the smaller girl, Bethany, in tow. Judy winced at the racket they were making but she didn't say anything, just gave her eldest daughter a resigned smile and a kiss on the cheek as she bounced inelegantly into the room.

'So, you decided to accept my invitation then?' Carin asked when she caught sight of Misty.

'What invitation?' Dylan interrupted before Misty had a chance to reply.

'To go and see the horses.'

'I've already shown her,' Dylan replied smugly. 'When you were stuck in school.'

'Enough, enough.' Judy held up her hands as if to keep brother and sister apart. If she had noticed Dylan's slip-up about school, she decided not to mention it. 'Sorry, Misty, they're always like this, at each other's throats, I'm afraid. Would you like to stay for dinner?'

Although Misty had already told her dad she might meet up with Carin that evening, she didn't want to get back too late. She bid a hasty farewell to them all, promising that she would bring her dad with her next time, and they would both stay for dinner.

As she made her way back to the house, Misty's head was spinning with new information. Fred was Dylan's *uncle*. That's how Dylan had almost got away with stealing the poor man's horse. He had seemed annoyed at first, but not incurably so. She wondered where Dylan went to school or if he went at all. She couldn't believe that Judy was his mum, and Carin and Bethany were his sisters. She wondered if they also knew the boy with the grey horse that she had seen on the high street the previous weekend. Perhaps she had made some new friends after all.

In the quiet of the early evening air, with only the sound of birdsong for company, Misty's thoughts turned uneasily back to her two oldest friends. She felt as if her phone was burning a hole in her pocket and could almost feel the messages building up, like a hundred sets of eyes watching her every move. She knew she would have to face Ruby and Jasmine eventually but hoped sleeping off an upset stomach would be enough of a reason to throw them off the scent for a little while longer.

'Did you visit the horses?' Dad asked as they sat down for another dinner of the same old pasta later that evening. Even after a couple of servings it was getting boring, and Misty thought longingly about the inviting smells that had been wafting out of the kitchen at Dylan's house.

'Just for a bit,' Misty said. 'I went over to Carin's, but I didn't stay very long. Judy was there, she said we should go round for dinner one evening. I mean if you want to—'

'Want to?' Dad exclaimed, causing Misty to jump in the air. She was feeling slightly on edge, aware of her every word, taking care not to accidentally spill out her secrets.

'I'd love to.' Dad was now gesturing towards the meal laid out on the table in front of them, as if to say anything was better than this.

Misty started to laugh, quietly at first, before her dad joined in and they were both giggling like hysterical teenagers. The air suddenly felt much clearer, as if the tension of the past few months had started to melt away.

'At least there's still some ice cream for dessert,' Dad said, as he took in huge gulps of air and tried to compose himself.

'Sounds great,' Misty replied, the widest of smiles spreading over her face. She felt in that moment that they were on the same page, united by a shared hatred of leftovers and a love of sweet treats. That together they could overcome anything, and that all that really mattered was that they still had each other whatever the future might bring.

Her phone buzzed again jolting her back to the present, and she glanced down at it briefly. The screen was lit up with a text from Ruby asking where she had been that day and why she wasn't replying to any of their messages. She quickly switched her phone onto silent before her dad could ask who it was from. She could feel her lies stacking up around her like a deck of cards that were waiting to scatter at any moment. Only the slightest of touches and they would all come fluttering down to land in an unruly pile at her feet.

CHAPTER TEN

Although she felt bad for deceiving her friends, Misty spent the next couple of days bunking off school to spend more time with Dylan and the horses. On Wednesday morning, she had sent Jasmine and Ruby a quick message to say she had a terrible stomach bug and headed down to the common to meet Dylan again. He showed her the morning routine of the yard; how to muck out Colin's stable, where his feed was kept and how to fill up his water bucket. Whilst they were grooming Colin, they talked more about Dylan's family and how they had come to live on the estate.

It seemed to Misty that everyone in Redbridge was related or knew each other in some way. What had at first appeared to be a harsh and desolate place to live, now seemed to be full of families and friendships; kin bound tightly by a thread of love, acceptance and support for one another. When Misty asked him about it, Dylan confided that his father, Thomas, had moved from the west coast of Ireland to work on the steelworks with Fred and had tragically been killed in an accident shortly after Bethany was born.

'I'm so sorry,' Misty said, blushing furiously at her mistake. She should have known to tread more carefully where missing family members were concerned.

'That's ok, it was a long time ago. Fred's like a surrogate father to me now.'

'My mum died a couple of years ago.' The words sprang from Misty's lips before she had time to think about them. 'I still miss her every day.'

'That must be tough,' Dylan replied, but instead of offering empty words of sympathy he said no more on the subject and continued pulling muck out of Colin's tangled feathers.

'It is,' Misty stated simply. With Dylan, she didn't feel she had to follow up with some sort of platitude about how she was doing all right now like she usually would when people asked her about her mother.

Colin snorted and pulled back on his lead rope. Even in the short time she had been around him, Misty had noticed what a stubborn character he was, with an obstinate streak as large as his owner's. Fred and Colin were like two peas in a pod; if horses could look like their humans, they certainly fit the bill. Most of the time Colin had a calm, placid nature but he did everything on his own terms, sometimes escaping from his makeshift stable by opening the bolt with his teeth or, on the opposite end of the scale, refusing to budge an inch.

'I saw a boy on a grey horse when I was out walking the other day.' The mysterious figure suddenly leapt into focus from a dusty corner of Misty's mind. She had been meaning to ask Dylan about him. If he was from the estate, they would surely have run into him by now.

'A *grey* horse?' Dylan asked quizzically. 'Are you sure?'

'I think so.' Misty hesitated as she tried to recall the events of the previous weekend. 'The horse was quite small, and the boy was about my age with dark blond hair.'

'There are no grey horses on the common,' Dylan replied. 'I suppose it's possible that they were just out for a ride. Perhaps they were visiting someone?'

'Maybe.'

Seemingly unconcerned, Dylan turned round and continued to brush Colin's mane. Misty was surprised that Dylan didn't know of the other boy or recognise the description of the small grey horse, but she pushed the thought away, and it was soon forgotten as they continued with the tasks of the day.

On Thursday, as they worked their way around the yard making sure everything was neat and tidy, Misty found out that Dylan's family were descended from Irish travellers and that was partly why Fred still lived in a caravan and refused to move into a house on the estate.

'That's why we all love horses so much,' he explained to her as they swept. 'It's in our blood.'

That afternoon, they were joined by Carin and watched as she constructed makeshift jumps out of old logs that were scattered on the common and soared over them fearlessly on her chestnut horse, Solo. Solo was an ex-racehorse who they had rehomed when he had to retire early due to an injury. Carin had nursed him back to health and he was now fit enough to compete at local events though he would never race again. This suited Carin fine as she wanted to be a professional showjumper when she was older.

Misty was quickly learning that the Murphy children had a very relaxed attitude when it came to school attendance as much as their mum tried to cajole them. Dylan wanted to do an apprenticeship the following year, so didn't see the point of academia, and was happy enough helping Fred with the horses and fixing things that were brought to his uncle to be mended.

That evening Misty decided to take up Judy's offer of dinner. When she checked her phone, she had a couple of messages from Ruby and Jasmine saying they were thinking of her and wishing her a speedy recovery, but she hoped that when she didn't answer they would assume she was still resting. She felt guilty for not inviting her dad as Judy had suggested on Tuesday evening, but she was worried someone might accidentally reveal what she had been doing with her time instead of going to school; she also wanted to keep her new friends to herself for a little while longer, revelling in the homely chaos of their family life.

'Ahh, there you are,' Judy called, as Misty and Dylan came through the back door that led straight into the kitchen. 'Good to see you again, Misty. You can both help Bethany with her homework and Carin can set the table while I sort all this out.'

Misty and Dylan sat down with Bethany in the living room and tried to help her figure out her spellings and work through her sums. For all the school he had apparently missed, Dylan was easily able to complete most of the younger girl's homework, even whilst Carin forced their elbows out of the way to place cutlery and plates down on the placemats in front of them.

'How do you spell stupendous?' Bethany asked and Carin laughed as Dylan tried and failed to come up with the correct answer.

'See, he's not very bright,' Carin told Misty spitefully.

Dylan scowled but Misty knew that he had been doing fine until that last spelling and wondered briefly if Carin was annoyed that Misty was spending so much time with her older brother instead of hanging around with her. *Perhaps we should try and include Carin a bit more*, she thought to herself, but from what she had seen so far, she wasn't sure how Dylan would feel about that, as they always seemed to be in competition with one another.

'Dinner's ready,' Judy called, as she came into the room and set down a large dish of steaming cottage pie at the centre of the table.

'This looks amazing,' Misty said politely.

'Oh, it's nothing much.' Judy expertly batted away the compliment as she sat down across from her. 'We grow all of the veg on Fred's allotment, you know.'

As soon as she mentioned his name, Fred appeared as if he had been summoned by the irresistible smell of cottage pie.

'Sorry I'm late, Colin got out again. That horse will be the death of me someday. You mark my words.'

Dylan quickly raised a fork to his mouth in a furtive attempt to hide the delight that had just crossed his face. Fred looked flustered and even Dylan could see that this probably wasn't the time to start playing on his nerves which were wound tightly like an expertly strung violin.

'Nice to see you again, Misty,' he said, as he took a deep breath and sat down beside her.

Misty smiled back at him, and a comfortable silence fell around the table as everyone tucked into their food. Misty was somewhat distracted by thoughts of her father who was probably sitting down to another bowl of leftovers right about now whilst she was here eating a flavoursome meal surrounded by welcoming people.

Once they had finished eating, Misty decided that it was time for her to head off. The food had settled heartily in her stomach, and she felt if she didn't leave now she might stay in the warmth of the Murphy's cramped living room for ever.

'Make sure you bring your dad with you next time,' Judy demanded. 'It'd be nice to see him again. You're both more than welcome, any time.'

'Thanks, I'll remind him,' Misty replied sheepishly, wondering how she would explain to her dad that she had been to dinner without him. Especially after the understanding they had come to over their pitiful meal on Monday evening. Her dad seemed to be spending most of his time filling out applications. She was certain he would have wanted to come with her if only she had given him the chance. Perhaps Fred might even be able to help him find some work around the estate.

'I'll walk you back,' Dylan said, jumping up from his seat.

'Ooh, lovebirds,' Carin teased, as she started making repulsively wet kissing noises and retching in mock disapproval.

'Don't be so rude, Carin,' Judy chided. 'Dylan's right to make sure Misty gets home safely.'

'As long as that's all he does,' Carin retorted.

Judy gave her a fierce glance of warning that would have stopped a herd of wild horses in their tracks.

Misty's ears turned a violent shade of red at the insinuation. She looked down, as if the answer to all of life's problems might appear on the empty plate in front of her.

'I'll be fine,' she mumbled as she pushed her seat back from the table and stumbled to her feet.

Dylan looked lost for words and gave his sister a treacherous glare. Carin at least had the decency to look slightly bashful as Judy sighed heavily and began to clear the plates from the table.

'Don't worry,' Fred jumped in to rescue her. 'I'll take you. *And* Dylan. We can check on the horses on the way back.'

'Well, I'm glad that's sorted,' Judy replied. 'Off you go before your sister has anything else to say about it.' She gave Dylan an encouraging nudge and leant over to give Misty a peck on the cheek in farewell. 'Ignore Carin, she's just jealous,' she whispered in Misty's ear.

'Mum—' Carin interjected. 'Don't be so embarrassing.'

'What?' Judy looked down at her eldest daughter, pretending to act surprised. 'Dylan was just doing the gentlemanly thing, there's no need to go causing a big scene.'

'Right, can we get going?' Fred called out impatiently as he struggled into his heavy sheepskin coat. 'I don't have forever to wait.'

Misty felt relieved as they said their goodbyes and were finally on the move, her breath turning to fog in the pitch-dark night air. After they had been walking for a few minutes, Misty turned to Dylan and asked, 'Do you think Carin really *is* jealous?'

Dylan paused for a moment as he considered the best response. 'She just doesn't like to be left out, that's all. Her bark's much worse than her bite.'

Misty was surprised at how sympathetic Dylan was towards Carin, especially after the way she seemed to have been treating him all evening. Perhaps she had misjudged their relationship; she had no siblings of her own to know if theirs was a regular one or not. Perhaps Dylan wouldn't mind if they asked Carin to spend time with them after all. Fred had hurried on ahead and was waiting for them on the corner of Misty's street, shuffling from foot to foot in a perfunctory attempt to keep warm.

'All right if we leave you here?' he asked once they had caught up. 'We'd better go and check that Colin hasn't made another break for it.'

Misty nodded her head in reply and started to make her way to her front door. The living-room lights were shining in the darkness and Misty wondered when she should ask Fred about her dad helping him with jobs around the estate. When she turned back, she saw that Dylan and Fred were already making their way back down the road towards the common and she knew the moment was lost.

'Night, Misty,' Dylan called out when he saw her looking at them and she waved, before walking into the house.

As she let herself in, Misty could hear the soft sound of music drifting from the speaker on the other side of the living room. It wasn't the usual boisterous rock music her father listened to but a soulful voice, rising and falling through peaks and valleys that instantly took Misty back to her younger self. She could feel her mother's warm hands on her arms as they danced together, could hear the delicate tinkle of her laughter like a windchime caught in a mild breeze. The force of the memory made her feel as though she had temporarily forgotten how to breathe.

Her dad was on the sofa gazing at a small pile of papers that were stacked neatly on the coffee table in front of him. He didn't seem to have noticed her come in and he looked so lonely sitting there on his own, that Misty felt terrible for leaving him instead of asking him to join her at Judy and Dylan's for dinner.

'What are you doing?' Misty asked, even as she continued to be absorbed by the music.

'Just listening to some of your mum's old CDs,' he said, attempting a reassuring smile that didn't quite reach his eyes. 'I was starting to get a bit worried about you.

You're meant to text me if you're going to be back later than planned.'

'What's all this?' Misty asked, gesturing to the mound of paperwork, not wanting to admit that she had been to the Murphys' without him.

'Just the latest selection of bills. Nothing for you to worry about,' Dad replied.

But Misty could tell by the look on his face that he was extremely worried, and if something was making him anxious then it was bound to have a negative effect on her too. Perhaps it was the familiar music transporting her to another time that made her realise they hadn't done anything fun, just the two of them, in a long time.

'Surely, there's something we can do?' Misty offered. 'Maybe we could sell something?'

Her brain ran over all the items that were currently in storage but whilst there were a few things that held a great deal of sentimental value she couldn't think of anything that was worth that much money.

'What about a car-boot sale?' Misty continued, remembering the ones they used to visit almost every weekend. Perhaps if they sold enough smaller items the money would start to add up.

'That's a good idea,' Dad replied. 'But I think we should give it a few more weeks before we start selling the family silver.'

'Silver?' Misty wondered if she had missed something of value in her mental catalogue of their possessions.

'It's just a turn of phrase,' her dad replied, chuckling to himself. 'I'm sure it won't come to that, anyway.'

CHAPTER ELEVEN

By Friday, Misty knew that she had to make an appearance at school. Missing three days was already pushing it and although her dad was preoccupied with his job search, she was sure he would start to suspect something the longer she didn't go in. Friday was also the evening of her sleepover at Jasmine's house and if she missed it, her friends were bound to realise there was more going on than the upset stomach she had texted them about on Wednesday morning.

The previous night, before she went to bed, Misty had sent the girls a cheery message saying that she was feeling much better and couldn't wait for the sleepover the next evening. She included a line of smiley face and heart emojis just to be on the safe side. Jasmine replied straightaway with an animated celebratory gif saying she couldn't wait to see her and was glad she was ok, but from Ruby there was radio silence which was odd as Ruby always had something to say.

Misty tried to ignore her growing sense of unease, and decided that whatever Ruby was thinking, she was sure everything would be fine once they were all in Jasmine's bedroom eating pizza, watching TikTok videos of cute kittens and gossiping about the boys in the year above and whether any of them were going to be asked to the disco at the end of the year.

The next day flew by as Misty struggled to concentrate on her lessons as she worried about facing her friends at the end of the day. She had purposely arrived just as the bell was ringing that morning, so she wouldn't have to face an interrogation at the beginning of the day. But before she had even had time to blink, it was home time, and Jasmine and Ruby were waiting for her by the school gates.

'Hello stranger,' Ruby offered, but she didn't sound too unhappy, it was Friday after all.

'I'm glad you're feeling better,' Jasmine countered. 'It must have been rotten being off sick for most of the week.'

Misty pushed down the wave of guilt she felt for misleading her friends and making them worry about her unnecessarily.

'I'm just glad I'm here now,' Misty said, swiftly moving the conversation forwards. 'I can't wait for tonight.'

'Me neither,' Ruby replied. 'Mum's given me twenty pounds so we can get pizza delivered.'

Misty wondered what Jasmine's mum and dad would have to say about that. They usually wanted the three girls to sit at the dining table and eat a proper home-cooked meal with them before they were allowed to escape to Jasmine's bedroom to watch TV. As if reading her mind, Jasmine gulped uncertainly.

'I think Mum's made a special meat-free lasagne with lentils that she's desperate for us to try,' she said.

'Yuck! What's lentils?' Ruby made a face. 'I'm sure we can persuade her that we'd much rather have pizza.'

'Maybe we should at least try the lasagne,' Misty cut in, trying to rescue the situation. 'If Ivy's gone to a lot of trouble. We can always order a pizza later if we're still hungry.'

Jasmine smiled gratefully.

'I suppose so,' Ruby replied, before adding naughtily, 'and I've got a secret stash of chocolate that I stole from the kitchen. Mum's going to kill me when she finds out I've taken it.'

The rest of the walk to Jasmine's was uneventful. Ruby was explaining at length what had happened in the rehearsals for *Romeo and Juliet* that week. Misty was glad of the distraction from discussing her pretend illness and didn't mind listening as Ruby debated the limited costume budget and whether there would be enough money for the wig, designer dress and *Devil Wears Prada*-style heels she envisaged for her Shakespearean debut.

When they reached Jasmine's traditional chocolate-box cottage, Ruby had hardly paused to take a breath and had moved on to describing the stunning visual effects that would be needed for a play that centred around death, but which would in fact, have no actual death in it at all.

'Not even a single body,' Ruby was despairing as the girls hurried into the house where Jasmine's mum waited patiently to hang up their coats.

'What's this about a puppy?' Ivy misheard.

Misty had always secretly adored Jasmine's cluttered, untidy home. There were piles of stuff on every available surface and leaning against the walls, threatening to topple over at any minute. Jasmine's mum, Ivy, seemed to ooze motherliness as if it was running through her veins, and although Jasmine found her overbearing at times, well most of the time, Misty found her immensely warm and welcoming.

'There is *no* body, that's the problem,' Ruby explained.

'Perhaps you could borrow Teddy?' Ivy offered, still totally at a loss as to what on earth the girls were talking about.

'I'm not sure there are any dogs in *Romeo and Juliet*,' Misty replied.

'It's for the school play, Mum,' Jasmine explained. 'The last thing they want is Teddy causing havoc and ruining the entire production. Remember what happened at Christmas?'

Ivy furrowed her brow for a second. 'That wasn't really his fault,' she said. 'He was just doing what any dog would have done given the situation.'

Teddy was Jasmine's Airedale terrier. He was a lively stray that Ivy had found at a rescue centre and had instantly fallen in love with. He was highly untrained and always getting into lots of trouble even though his long face made him look far wiser and more superior than he actually was.

'Where is Teddy anyway?' Jasmine asked cautiously.

'In the garden. I had to lock him outside when he tried to make off with my lasagne.'

The three girls looked at each other and burst into a fit of uncontrollable sniggers. It was just like the unruly mutt to try and eat their dinner.

'Now go and sit down,' Ivy said. 'It's almost ready.'

The lentil lasagne-tasting passed without disaster and Misty thought it had actually been quite a success. It was nowhere near as bad as the time Jasmine's dad, Clive, had made them try bulgur wheat for the first time and it turned out to have the consistency of lumpy cold porridge with dramatically less flavour, and that was saying something. Even Ruby had eaten most of tonight's meal which was high praise indeed. Most of Ruby's mum's cooking comprised of M&S ready meals and takeaways. She was a single parent who ran her own law firm and didn't have much time to spend on creating nutritious home-cooked meals. It was usually down to Ruby to fend for herself most evenings and make something for her younger brother, Jason, whilst their mum was working on her latest case, which often resorted to her ordering from Deliveroo.

Once the girls had been excused from the table, they ran up to Jasmine's bedroom with the recently liberated Teddy bounding close behind. Once they had shut the door firmly, Ruby rounded on Misty.

'Aren't you going to tell us where you *really* were all week?' she asked defiantly.

'I told you, I had a stomach bug,' Misty replied, stroking Teddy's ears uneasily. 'I didn't feel well enough to come in.'

'And last weekend? You never did tell us how the decorating turned out. Perhaps we could see a photo of this marvellous makeover?'

Misty stared at the carpet beneath her polka-dot socks, as if the answer might be written in the pile. She could feel her stomach churning anxiously and wished the ground would open and she could disappear completely.

'Ruby,' Jasmine tried to placate her, 'why don't you just drop it? Can't you see you're upsetting her?'

'We're meant to be *best friends*,' Ruby continued. 'Best friends are meant to tell each other everything. And I *know* there's something you're not telling us.'

When Misty still didn't reply, Jasmine said, 'Why don't we just enjoy tonight? We've still got the disco to discuss. And my triathlon. I need some ideas for my sponsorship. How much money do you think I should aim for?'

'At least five hundred pounds,' Ruby suggested, her outburst momentarily forgotten, ever the ambitious lawyer's daughter.

Misty knew that eventually she was going to have to own up to her friends. They had both guessed that something was wrong, and Ruby would be like a cunning hound following the scent of an outsmarted fox until she told them what it was. But she wasn't ready to tell them yet, not whilst there was still a chance, however small it might seem, that her dad would find a new job soon and she'd never have to admit what had happened to them.

'Please tell us what's wrong?' Ruby said as she turned back to Misty, her voice slightly calmer now.

'There's nothing to tell,' Misty said, her voice wobbling as she spoke. 'I've just had a weird week, but things will be back to normal now, you'll see.'

CHAPTER TWELVE

When Misty returned home on Saturday evening the house was silent. She'd spent the day at the shopping centre with Ruby and Jasmine and everything had felt almost ordinary. There had been a flash mob in town and Ruby had insisted on joining in with the dancing, copying the increasingly complex moves with ease and making up her own when all else failed. Jasmine was horrified at the thought of being made to get involved, whilst Misty shuffled self-consciously from side to side in a reluctant attempt to humour Ruby.

Now she was back in Redbridge and a world away from the hubbub of the town centre on its main shopping day. The house was dark, and as she entered the living room thoughts of unpaid bills crashed into her mind. She wondered how things could change so quickly, her dad's high spirits of one day dissolving into worry and fear the next.

'Cup of tea, Dad?' Misty asked, trying to act as if everything was fine as she switched on the stark glare of the overhead spotlights in the kitchen. It felt like an interrogation chamber, and Misty longed for the warm, comforting glow of the golden lighting that ran under the cabinets and illuminated the worktops in their old home.

Her dad made no attempt to reply and continued to stare resolutely at the table in front of him. Misty turned on the kettle and flinched as it came to the boil, breaking through the heavy atmosphere that had settled over the room. She found two dirty mugs in the sink and scrubbed at them furiously as she struggled to decide what to do next.

'Dad?' Misty persisted, nudging his arm gently when still he made no response.

Misty dried the cups and finished making the tea, placing a mug lightly in front of her dad who ignored it completely. It was as if she wasn't even there.

'The school called on Friday,' her dad said eventually, his words catching Misty completely off guard.

'The school?' she repeated back at him, a hot flush that wasn't caused by the tea rising in her cheeks.

'Yes, they wanted to check whether you were still contagious, said it sounded like a nasty bug you'd picked up.'

Misty's gaze met her dad's across the kitchen and she felt her eyes fill with tears. It was as though all of the pressure she'd been under since the move was surging out of her in an unstoppable tide of frustration.

Before she could stop herself, she told him everything; how upset she'd been to leave behind the house she'd grown up in, how she hadn't been able to tell her friends the truth about what had happened, how she had been bunking off school to spend time with Dylan and the horses rather than facing up to her problems.

'You don't need the old house to remember her, you know,' Dad said as he touched his hand to his heart. 'Your memories will always be with you, they're a part of you, a part that will never leave your side.'

'Why don't you ever talk about Mum?' Misty asked, feeling a seam that had been stitched tightly shut opening for the first time in a while.

'It's difficult,' he admitted as he looked her directly in the eye. 'I'm sorry if you've felt like you can't talk to me about things, especially your mum. I miss her too, you know.'

'I'm sorry about school,' Misty ventured, her voice shaking slightly as she spoke. 'Am I grounded?'

'No, you're not grounded,' Dad replied firmly. 'Just promise me you'll speak to me next time instead of letting things get on top of you like this. I'm sorry if I've seemed preoccupied recently.'

'I will, I promise.' Misty gave him a watery smile that didn't quite reach her eyes.

'And Misty, for what it's worth, I think you should talk to your friends. They'll understand but they can't help you unless you let them in.'

*

Misty left the house on Sunday morning and went to look for Dylan down by the common. She still wasn't sure how she could make things up to her dad, and she wondered if Dylan might be able to help her. Although she hadn't been friends with him long, she was already starting to find him easier to be with than either Ruby or Jasmine. His unquestioning presence put her instantly at ease and he understood how it felt to lose someone unexpectedly who you thought would be around for ever. Although she was keeping secrets from him too, he was part of her present whilst Ruby and Jasmine belonged to the old Misty, whom she was starting to feel increasingly distant from the more time she spent in Redbridge.

Dylan wasn't around. Amidst the browns and oranges of the clay-coloured horses that were usually there, Misty noticed a flash of silver on the horizon. As she got closer, she saw that the shiny coin-coloured coat belonged to a small, sturdy dapple-grey horse who snorted suspiciously and shook its long silvery mane as she approached.

To Misty, the animal looked like something out of a fairy tale, and although his head only reached just past her shoulder, he had the presence of a much larger being. As she watched him, he stamped his hoof impatiently as if asking what she was waiting for.

'You've found him then?' A loud voice startled Misty and she turned to see Carin standing beside her. 'Bit of a looker, that one, isn't he?' she continued. 'Bolshy, mind.'

'He's wonderful,' Misty managed to stutter in reply as she reached her hand out tentatively to brush the silvery horse with her fingers as if he might be a phantom standing in front of her. His coat was as shiny as a chocolate bar wrapper.

'That's settled. You can look after him,' Carin replied. 'We don't know his name. Fred reckons he was dumped here last night. I've been calling him Storm. On account of his looks and his personality.' She cackled. 'What do you think?'

Like Dylan, his sister had the same old-fashioned way of speaking, though her accent was much more pronounced, as if she also had grown up too quickly. She had the same freckled complexion, but her eyes were much darker and set slightly wider apart. Her eyebrows were raised expectantly as she waited for Misty's response.

'I don't know... if I have time to... look after a horse,' Misty stammered.

'Well, for a start he's a pony, he's about twelve hands high, but he's stocky enough to carry a skinny thing like you, I'd say.'

Although Misty had been slightly afraid of Carin at first, the more time they spent together, the more she got used to her straightforward manner. Maybe this proposal to look after the pony was in fact a peace offering and, if that was the case, Misty felt inclined to accept it. She took a deep breath and cast her eyes over the majestic little pony once again. It was in that moment that she realised she had seen him before. He pawed the ground and looked at her expectantly.

'OK,' she replied. 'I'll do it if you show me how. But I think I know who this pony belongs to.'

'They obviously don't want him if they've just left him here,' Carin replied indifferently. 'You may as well take care of him for now.'

Misty was almost one hundred per cent certain that this was the same horse, well, pony, that she had seen when she had first arrived in Redbridge, being ridden perilously down the high street. She briefly wondered what had happened to the boy who had been riding him that day but as Carin had said, he must not have been too bothered if, with no explanation given, the pony had suddenly ended up here.

By the time Dylan appeared a couple of hours later, Carin had already shown Misty the basics of how to take care of Storm. There was no mucking out to do as, aside from Colin, the ponies lived out on the hillside all year round, but Misty learnt how to brush Storm's already sparkling coat and pick out his feet to make sure there weren't any stones causing him discomfort. Carin also showed her how to fill up the water trough at the bottom of the field and where the hay was stored, in a shed by Fred's caravan, for when there wasn't enough grass in the winter to feed them.

'What's all this then?' Dylan asked.

They had tied Storm and Carin's horse, Solo, up together in the concrete yard in front of Fred's caravan. Misty had been so engrossed in brushing out Storm's long flowing tail that she hadn't even noticed that Dylan was there until he had spoken.

'This is the horse... I mean... the pony I was telling you about,' Misty gasped. 'The one I saw in town the other day.'

'Someone's left him here and Misty's volunteered to look after him,' Carin said, gesturing towards the small grey pony. 'I'm just showing her what's what.'

'Volunteered? Or been coerced?' Dylan smirked as he turned to Misty. 'I thought you didn't like horses that much?'

'I don't... I didn't...' Misty stammered weakly, before recovering herself. 'But Storm's only a pony.'

'Well said.' Fred had appeared and was slowly making his way down the steps that were built into the side of his caravan. The small metal frame shook dangerously as it struggled under the large man's weight. 'It's good to see you taking an interest. I knew you'd come round eventually.'

'But I never—' Misty began.

'Said anything?' Dylan offered. 'You don't have to. Fred thinks he knows everything, you see. He's got psychic powers. It's a traveller thing apparently. Best not to ask.'

'How's your dad getting on?' Fred continued, as if his nephew hadn't spoken. His small eyes held within them a disconcertingly laser-sharp gaze.

'Fine.' Misty blinked nervously. Fred was examining her more closely now, and he nodded, then shook his large, bald head as if coming out of a trance. Misty felt as if he could see straight through her words, under her skin and directly into her mind. She could tell from the look he gave her that he didn't believe a word of it but just when she thought he was going to challenge her, Carin – seemingly unaware of the silent duel currently playing out between them – swiftly came to her rescue.

'Right, time for your first ride, then?' She gestured towards Storm's broad back. 'On you get.'

Forgetting Fred for a moment, Misty replied, 'I can't just get on. Can I? What about a saddle? And I've got nothing to hold on to.'

'Sadly, castoffs don't come with any tack,' Carin quipped. 'You'll just have to make do with a headcollar and a lead rope, and go bareback. You'll be fine.'

Misty looked round for someone to come to her rescue. Carin was getting impatient. Fred looked as though his mind was elsewhere. Dylan was observing her with one eyebrow raised as if daring her to do it, then relented slightly when he saw the helpless look on her face.

'I'll go get Colin's bridle,' he said. 'But you'll have to make do without a saddle, we don't have one small enough to fit him.'

Once Dylan returned with the bridle and had adjusted the cheek pieces so it was small enough to fit Storm, Carin put her hands under Misty's knee and thrust her into the air before she had time to protest. She felt a strange sense of vertigo as she flew upwards but then she was settled precariously on Storm's back, her knees struggling to grip his slippery coat. The thud of her inelegant landing made Storm jump forward, but luckily Dylan was still holding on to him and managed to quickly settle him again.

'Whoa, it's ok, little man,' he said as he stroked Storm comfortingly on the nose. 'Try to relax your knees and grip with your calves,' he advised Misty. 'If you're tense, he'll feel it.'

'Maybe I should get off?' Misty suggested. It was all very well being told to relax but Storm's back was as slick as an ice-skating rink, and she was struggling to keep her balance.

'Try holding on to his mane, just there, by his withers.' Dylan gestured to a small bump, a bit like an Adam's apple, that protruded from Storm's back just in front of where she was sitting.

Misty grabbed a chunk of mane and tried her best to keep still. As her knees relented and her back started to straighten, she found herself able to sit up and look forward over Storm's pricked ears.

'That's it,' Dylan encouraged as he started to walk Storm slowly onward. 'You're doing it. See, it's easy when you know how.'

Misty felt herself smiling despite herself. Storm was only moving at a snail's pace, but she felt as if she was floating on air.

'What do you think?' Dylan persisted gently. 'Do you like it?'

'Yes, I think I do,' Misty replied. 'One thing though, we're going to have to come up with a better name.'

After the lesson was over, they turned the horses back out onto the common and were leaning on the fence watching them graze peacefully in the pink hazy light of an early evening sunset. Bethany and Judy had shown up a bit later, and they all watched as Judy led Bethany around the field on the back of her Shetland pony, Buttons. Now everyone else had gone home and Misty and Dylan were the only ones left watching the horses as they settled in for a night on the hillside.

'Sparkle,' Misty stated firmly.

When Dylan looked at her blankly, Misty continued, looking out at the little grey pony who stood on the other side of the fence. 'His name. Storm doesn't suit him at all. He's much more of a Sparkle in my opinion.'

Dylan looked thoughtful for a second before his perfectly round face broke into a broad smile.

'What?' Misty said, as he continued to examine her with an amused grin on his face. 'Don't you like it?'

'You can call him Potato for all I care,' Dylan replied playfully. 'I'm surprised to see you taking such an interest. Just don't get too attached.'

'Well, he's my responsibility now,' Misty countered. 'And I want him to have a good name.'

The small pony snorted as if in agreement.

'Fine, Sparkle it is,' Dylan agreed. 'But don't say I didn't warn you when his owner turns up wanting him back. Now, I'd better get going before Mum puts the dinner on the table. She'll be mad if I'm late. Do you want to come? I'm sure she wouldn't mind one extra mouth to feed.'

Misty hesitated. There was nothing she would like more than to join Judy, Dylan and the others. But the thought of her dad spending another evening on his own made the decision for her. Although she hadn't been grounded this time, she felt that she should be on her best behaviour.

'I can't tonight. I promised my dad I'd come home. He's making something special.' The lie slipped easily off her tongue. 'Next time though.'

'OK, next time, then. And don't forget to bring your dad with you. Mum will take it as a personal insult if he doesn't accept her invitation soon.' Dylan slowly walked away, watching her as he went. 'See you around then.'

'See you around,' she called softly.

CHAPTER THIRTEEN

By the end of term, Misty had settled into a new routine. At school she hung out with Ruby and Jasmine as normal, and she spent her evenings on the common with Dylan, Carin and the horses. Luckily, Ruby had rehearsals for the school play after school most days and Jasmine was too engrossed in her triathlon training to notice Misty rushing off to meet her new friends as soon as the bell rang at the end of each day.

The final day of school came round quickly, and the girls had gathered to help Ruby put the finishing touches to her costume. The play would take place that afternoon and all of the parents, guardians and family members were invited to come and watch the performance. After they had helped Ruby into her dress, Mr Stevens, Ruby's drama teacher, poked his head round the curtain to where they were sitting backstage.

'You're on in five,' he told Ruby as he gave her an encouraging thumbs-up.

The girls wished Ruby good luck and made their way into the school hall, which was jampacked with students and relatives who had come to see the show. Jasmine waved at her dad; although she wasn't performing in the play, he was there to review it for the local newspaper. They could see Ruby's mum, Sheila, near the exit, busily tapping on her phone. The banner that the girls had painted together hung proudly over the stage, *Romeo and Juliet* spelled out in glittery pink lettering.

'It looks great.' Misty nudged Jasmine and gestured towards the makeshift balcony where Ruby was about to make her appearance. 'Very professional. Ruby will be pleased.'

'I'm so glad we're all friends again.' Jasmine smiled broadly. 'I missed all three of us hanging out together.'

'Me too.' Misty hugged Jasmine tightly and settled into her seat. The lights were dimming, and the play was about to begin. 'I just hope it all goes to plan, or there'll be hell to pay.'

Misty needn't have worried; the play was a resounding success and there was unanimous agreement amongst the audience that Ruby made an unusually feisty and resourceful Juliet. She was grinning from ear to ear as she recalled Ruby's obvious reluctance to take her own life because of her lover's death. Even Ruby had to concede that the eye-rolling was taking it a step too far and had caused raucous laughter from the audience.

'Perhaps stick to the script next time,' Mr Stevens had quipped as the girls were waiting by the back door.

'I just don't think tragedy is for me,' Ruby had announced, unfazed as ever by her teacher's critique. 'Comedy's more my thing.'

'I'm sure Shakespeare would agree. Perhaps we'll try *A Midsummer Night's Dream* next year. Enjoy the holidays!' This time it was Mr Stevens turn to raise his eyes skyward as he sent the girls on their way.

'Are you sure you can't come to mine tonight?' Ruby turned to Misty as soon as Mr Stevens had gone.

'Sorry,' Misty replied guiltily. 'I promised I'd spend some time with my dad.'

'Don't worry,' Jasmine said. 'We'll see plenty of each other over the holidays, won't we?'

'Of course, we will,' Misty answered. 'See you next week!'

Misty felt bad for having deceived her friends but as she ran towards the common to meet Dylan as she had planned to that morning, those thoughts quickly melted away. She couldn't wait to practise her riding with Sparkle and Carin, and to spend more time with everyone in Redbridge over the holiday with no school to get in the way for two entire weeks.

'I'm free,' Misty shouted, raising her arms over her head in celebration as she burst into the yard where the others were waiting. But before they could answer, Fred appeared from his caravan his brow furrowed in anger.

'What's wrong?' Dylan asked, serious for once.

'There were some men from the council out on the common this morning,' Fred replied darkly. 'Taking photos of the horses... measuring things...'

'But why would they do that?' Carin said, nervously twirling a piece of her long dark hair between her fingertips.

Misty gasped when she thought of what might happen to Sparkle and the others. 'Do you think they're going to take the horses away?'

'The horses belong to us and the common is public land, but they were definitely up to something,' Fred continued. 'And I'm as good as damned if I'm going to let them get away with it.'

Misty had never seen Fred look so angry, it was a stark contrast to the mock fighting he and Dylan undertook most of the time. His mouth was set in a firm, obstinate line which reminded Misty of Colin when he was given an instruction he had no intention of following. Misty couldn't possibly imagine why the council would take an interest in the scruffy bit of land that was the horses' home. Perhaps Fred had been mistaken somehow and it was all perfectly innocent, and they were just embarking on some sort of routine maintenance work.

'It might be nothing,' Dylan said uncertainly. 'But it's more likely to be something.'

'Something bad,' Carin agreed.

'Something terrible,' Fred echoed.

'Whatever it is, we'll stop them,' Misty replied. 'But there's no point in worrying until we know for sure.'

Misty had no reason to fear the council, but Fred knew the prejudices the travelling community often faced at the hands of authority. They'd been lucky to have spent the last ten years relatively settled by blending into the background, but Fred was sure that if the council wanted them gone, they would be and there was nothing they could do about that. Fred made his way back to his caravan and all thoughts of their planned riding lesson were abandoned.

'We'd better get going,' Carin said. That evening both Misty and her dad were invited to the Murphys' house for dinner and Misty's stomach filled with fluttering creatures when she thought about introducing her dad to Dylan for the first time.

When they got back to the Murphys' home, they found Misty's dad was already inside. He had even put on a crisp white shirt, the kind he used to wear when he went to the office, and Misty was relieved that he still wanted to make an effort despite everything he had been going through recently.

'Hi, Dad.' She smiled warmly and took his arm as she introduced him to her new friends. They had been getting on well ever since their conversation about Misty's mother and the move, and Misty hoped he would extend the same warm feeling towards Dylan.

'Hi Misty,' Judy called out, her hands wrestling with a chicken. 'So glad you could both make it this time.'

'Thanks for the invitation,' her dad replied. 'I don't think Misty can take much more of my cooking.'

'Hey, I like your cooking,' Misty joked. 'It's just not that varied... some of the time!'

Misty didn't want to raise the subject of the foodbank in front of Judy, even though she was the one who had helped them in the first place, or to think about the pile of bills still waiting for them on the table at home. She was hoping they could have a fun evening, her dad finally spending time with all her friends from the estate.

'Go and sit down.' Judy gestured towards the living room. 'There's not much space so best to get a spot before my lot beat you to it.'

As they entered the living room, Dylan, Carin and Bethany hardly looked up as they perched on the sofa fighting over an iPad, so Misty and her dad took their seats at the table as Judy had suggested. When the food was ready, they all piled over, with her dad taking Fred's usual spot.

'Where is he?' Dylan asked, gesturing towards his uncle's seat, oblivious to Misty's concern when it came to him meeting her dad for the first time.

Judy's brow furrowed. 'He's still worrying about those men he saw down at the common this morning. It's been hard to tear him away.'

'What's this?' Misty's dad asked innocently, unaware of the trouble that Fred thought might be heading their way.

'Oh, it's just Fred. He's got it into his head that the common's under threat and he's keeping a constant watch over it until he's proved otherwise,' Judy explained. 'I'm sure it will all come to nothing. Anyway, what about you? How's the job search going? Any luck finding something?'

Misty's dad's eyes darkened briefly at the mention of work, and he promptly brushed the question away and proposed a toast to the chef. As they raised their water glasses towards Judy, Misty realised he was too proud to ever admit that they needed any further help. At least he was distracted from paying too much attention to Dylan.

Misty needn't have worried; overall, the dinner had been a resounding success. Once the thrust of the conversation moved away from him, her dad had seemed completely at ease, probably due to Judy's excellent hosting skills. Dylan had been on his best behaviour and without Fred there to annoy, he didn't make any snide remarks at all. In fact, she had been having such a good time, she had neglected to message Ruby and Jasmine, so, as soon as she got home and went up to her room, she sent them a quick message asking how they were doing and arranging to meet up the next day.

During the first week of the Easter break, Misty and Sparkle became inseparable. After spending the first day of the holiday in town with her friends, Misty spent every spare moment she had strengthening her bond with the sturdy little pony and by the final few days of the holiday, once she had mastered walk, trot and canter effectively, Carin decided it was time she learned how to jump.

'Are you sure I'm ready?' Misty asked nervously, not quite certain that she wanted to go along with the plan. She sat astride Sparkle in a saddle they had borrowed from the owner of one of the other horses that was kept on the common so at least she was feeling more secure in that respect.

'We'll start off with poles on the ground,' Carin commanded. 'It'll be easy, don't worry. You just have to trot over them, make sure to look straight ahead and give Sparkle a little nudge in the side, so he knows when to pick up his feet.'

Misty glanced over at Dylan, who was watching the action with a bemused expression on his face. 'You'll be fine,' he said with a reassuring smile. 'I know you can do it.'

Misty took a deep breath and aimed Sparkle at the row of poles Carin had laid out at equal distances along the ground. She coaxed him into a slow trot and stared between his ears, completely focused on the task ahead. When she got closer, she squeezed his sides and Sparkle merrily picked up his hooves and danced lightly over the poles like a show pony.

'See, he knows exactly how it's done,' Carin called out, the satisfaction clear in her voice.

Misty practised going over the poles a couple more times, her confidence growing as Sparkle continued to show off his exemplary skills. He seemed to be enjoying it too, tossing his head and snorting with every dainty step they took over them.

'Right, now you've got the hang of it.' Carin walked over to the last pole and propped it up with a brick at each end. 'Now try that.'

It was a tiny jump, only half a foot high at best but to Misty it felt as if she was soaring over the moon. As the afternoon progressed the jumps got slowly higher until they were effortlessly clearing a crossbar that seemed absolutely ginormous to Misty but was probably only about two foot high.

Just as she was pushing the small, grey pony into a canter and turning to face the middle of the jump, Sparkle came crashing to a halt at the last moment, sending Misty flying over his head to land inelegantly on the other side of it.

'At least *you* got over,' Carin snorted. 'Are you ok?'

Sparkle had paused stock still, peering into the bushes on the other side of the common and Misty could have sworn that she saw a flash of movement in the hedgerows. *Is someone watching us?* But when she turned back the vision was gone and Sparkle was looking at her with a forlorn expression in his eyes.

'I'm fine,' Misty replied, shaking off the feeling of unease that had temporarily settled over her. 'I thought I saw something in the trees, that's all.'

As Misty stood up and brushed herself down, checking gingerly for any aches and pains, Dylan strode off in the direction of the undergrowth where Misty had pointed.

'There's no one there,' he confirmed. 'Sparkle must have got spooked by a bird or something. Maybe that's what you saw?'

'Must have been,' Misty replied, shaking her head in embarrassment. She walked over to Sparkle, giving him a rub on the nose to show she hadn't taken his behaviour personally. *Fancy getting frightened by a bird,* she thought. Fred's talk of the threat to the common must have got to her more than she had imagined.

CHAPTER FOURTEEN

All too soon the Easter holiday was over and Misty was back at school. However, when she reached the playground at half past eight there was no sign of either Ruby or Jasmine. Everything else seemed fine, the school yard was full of loud chatter and the thud of a football being passed back and forth reverberated around her, but still she could feel her heartbeat racing while time seemed to slow down.

Just as she was scanning the sea of faces, searching for her friends in the crowd, a loud, unmistakable voice shouted, 'That's her, the one I told you about,' and then everything seemed to speed up, as if someone had pressed fast forward, and suddenly Ruby was standing directly in front of her, pointing her finger accusingly in Misty's face.

'Why didn't you tell us?' she demanded angrily. 'We had to find out from some random boy in Year Eleven.'

'Tell you what?' Misty replied, her brain struggling to catch up with her mouth.

'Don't pretend you don't know what I'm talking about, you've been lying to us for months. No wonder you've been avoiding us recently.'

'I didn't lie,' Misty answered meekly, wishing the ground would open beneath her feet. It was true that aside from arranging a brief trip into town at the start of the holiday, she hadn't replied to any of her friends' messages since then. She had been so busy with Sparkle and the others in Redbridge that she had found it all too easy to forget about them completely.

'Someone saw you. Said they saw you. In Redbridge. With your dad. They say you've been living up there for weeks.'

By now a small crowd had gathered around the girls, desperate to know what all the raised voices were about. Misty wanted to run but she was trapped by the ocean of bodies that swayed back and forth watching them as if their disagreement was a spectator sport. Misty opened her mouth to say something, to protest her innocence, but she had no words; her dad had been right, there was no excuse for why she had hidden the truth from her best friends.

'Well?' Ruby persisted. 'Is it true?'

She was staring pointedly at Misty, waiting for an explanation and so were all the other pupils who were holding their collective breath, their eyes burning holes into her skin. Misty felt all the guilt and shame of the last few weeks rising as it threatened to swallow her whole. She was totally exhausted. She couldn't have escaped the claustrophobic crowd even if she had wanted to. Their bodies pressed in on her, holding her silently to account.

'Yes,' she spluttered, 'Redbridge. It's true.'

Ruby gave her a look of such loathing that Misty felt a wave of nausea crash through her stomach. She felt as if she couldn't breathe, as if the weight of the crowd surrounding them was pressing down on her windpipe as she gasped desperately for air. Her legs turned jelly-like beneath her and she crumpled to the ground. Just as she felt sure she would be left lying in a heap on the floor of the playground, she felt someone reach down and grab her hand.

Misty opened her eyes and saw Jasmine, her white-blonde hair framing her face like a halo. She took hold of Jasmine's arm with her other hand and struggled unsteadily to her feet. Once Jasmine drew herself up to her full height she could push easily through the crowd, who were now losing interest and parted to let the girls through. Misty could see that Ruby was still watching but she made no attempt to join them. She turned and strode in the other direction, towards the science block, whilst Jasmine and Misty walked cautiously towards a bench on the other side of the yard.

'I understand why you didn't want to tell us,' Jasmine offered, as she lowered Misty gently onto the bench.

Misty was mortified. It was nice of Jasmine to try and empathise, but she could never understand what it was like to be so uncomfortable that you had to conceal where you lived from your best friends.

'I didn't mean to lie to you both.' Misty exhaled. 'There's just been so much going on recently and I didn't want to tell you why we had moved. That Dad lost his job. I was hoping if he found a new one everything would go back to normal, and I'd never have to tell you about Redbridge. But the truth is, I've made friends there, real friends, who don't judge me for where I live or what my dad does. If Ruby can't understand that—'

'Don't worry about Ruby. She's just annoyed that you didn't tell us.' Jasmine smiled. 'And I can't wait to meet your new friends.'

'Thanks.' Misty managed to smile weakly but inside she was in turmoil. Her thoughts rushed from one place to another unable to settle on anything. Her dad. Redbridge. Dylan. Sparkle. She wanted to leave the playground for good. She couldn't wait to get back to her new friends in Redbridge, who understood that life wasn't always easy, but didn't ask too many questions and seemed willing to accept people just the way they were. As she tried to explain her true feelings to Jasmine, she realised that she was no longer embarrassed to live on the estate but instead that feeling had flipped like a pancake and it was herself she felt ashamed of, for ever doubting that Redbridge could be a place she felt proud to call home.

When Misty got back to Redbridge that evening, she ran straight to the common to find Dylan. He was waiting by the fence exactly where she had left him the previous day, as if he had been there ever since and hadn't moved a single inch.

'What's wrong?' Dylan asked when he saw the mournful expression on Misty's face. He raised his eyebrows upwards in his usual ironic fashion.

'Everyone knows,' Misty managed to splutter as she struggled to catch her breath.

'Knows what?'

Misty remembered with a start that she had also been keeping the truth from Dylan. That she had told him she was only visiting family in Redbridge, and she would only be there temporarily. She was beginning to lose track of all the different omissions and half-truths she had been spinning, tangled in a web of her own making. At least she had told him the truth about her mum, that was one less thing to try and conceal.

She took a deep breath and before she could think better of it, she blurted out, 'Everyone at school knows that I live here now. One of the older kids found out and told everyone. I'm not staying with family. I'm sorry I didn't tell you. My dad lost his job and we had to move. We had to leave our home and come here, to Redbridge. Only I thought it *would* be temporary. I thought we'd move back as soon as Dad found a new job—'

'Misty. Misty, it's ok,' Dylan interjected, cutting her off midsentence. 'I already know.'

'You know?' Misty stuttered. 'What do you mean you know? Why didn't you—"

'Say something?' Dylan interrupted again. 'Because I knew if you weren't telling me the whole truth there must be a good reason for it. I knew that if you wanted me to know, you'd tell me in your own time. There was no point trying to force it out of you before you were ready to share it. But whatever Carin might tell you, I'm not completely stupid. I knew you and your dad weren't just visiting.'

Misty couldn't believe how well Dylan was taking all this. It was the total opposite of how Ruby had reacted at school earlier that day. She knew she didn't deserve his friendship after the way she had judged Redbridge and all the people who lived here, and resolved to be a better friend to him from now on.

'I thought that if I told the truth, people would look down on me,' Misty confessed. 'I thought if I kept quiet, I could fix everything, and no one would ever need to know.'

'No one here will judge you,' Dylan said confidently. 'Ever. Not for just being who you are.'

'I realise that now,' Misty replied miserably. 'Everything is such a mess. I've fallen out with one of my best friends. Dad still hasn't found a job. It'll take a miracle to fix everything.'

'I think you should try talking to Fred,' Dylan offered. 'Maybe he can speak to your dad. He always has odd jobs that need doing around the estate and I'm sure he'd be more than happy to have an extra pair of hands.'

'Maybe,' Misty replied. She had been wondering if Fred might be able to help. It was definitely worth a try.

'And don't worry about your friend. I'm sure, if she's a proper friend, she'll come round and forgive you soon. You just need to let the dust settle a little bit first.'

'Thanks,' Misty said weakly. 'I better get home, but I'll speak to Fred soon, I promise.'

'Let's go in the morning. I'll come with you.'

'I've got school in the morning.'

'Like you said, you're not exactly popular at school at the minute.'

'But I can't just miss it, I promised Dad I wouldn't skip any more school.'

'One more day won't hurt,' Dylan replied with a grin. 'I hardly ever go to school, and I turned out all right, didn't I?'

Misty was starting to wonder if life would ever feel normal again. She couldn't believe that only a few months ago she was blindly following her old routine, oblivious to the huge upheaval that was charging straight towards her. Everything had changed now, and Dylan was right, one last day off school couldn't hurt. *Could it?* Especially if it was to help her dad. Surely he would understand.

'OK, I'll see you tomorrow,' she said, decision finally made. She still wasn't sure it was the right thing to do but anything was better than having to face Ruby and everyone else at school the next morning.

'Good, see you here at 8.30,' Dylan said, giving her his widest ear-to-ear grin. 'Don't be late.'

With that parting shot, Dylan turned and started ambling across the common towards home. Just as he was about to disappear, Misty shouted after him.

'How did you know I'd come find you this evening?'

'Just a feeling I had. You know what my family are like.' He gave a gesture that looked like he was conjuring magic from out of a hat.

Misty turned and started heading in the opposite direction. She couldn't help smiling at what Dylan had said, but as she got closer and saw that the house was still in darkness despite the lengthening shadows of the early evening, her smile turned into a frown. Whatever was waiting for her on the other side of the door, at least she had her plan with Dylan to put into practise the following morning.

She opened the door and crept slowly through the dark living room and into the empty kitchen. As she turned on the light, she saw that the kitchen table was covered in a pile of unwashed dishes. There was no sign of Dad. *Perhaps he's at a job interview,* she thought hopefully.

She found a tin of tomato soup, and wrinkling her nose in distaste, poured it into a pan to warm through. Once it was ready, she ate quickly, trying not to breathe in the sickly, sweet scent as she swallowed. It was probably for the best that Dad wasn't home yet, Misty reflected. At least she could go up to her room and avoid having to answer any potential questions about school the next day.

CHAPTER FIFTEEN

The next morning when Misty arrived at the common at 8.30am exactly, Dylan was already waiting for her as promised. As she got closer, her face broke into a grin at the sight of his open, freckly face and the broad smile that was almost a mirror image of her own.

'Ready then?' Dylan shouted once she was in earshot.

'Not really,' Misty admitted. 'Dad's going to be fuming if he finds out I've missed school again.'

'Don't worry. He's not going to find out. I can do most of the talking if you want, you can just back me up. Maybe add a few tears, make Fred feel sorry for you. That sort of thing should work.'

Misty wasn't so sure she could cry on command. As they walked over to Fred's caravan, she started to wonder if they were making a mistake bothering him at all. But before she had a chance to back out, Fred's large round head appeared, followed by his even larger round body. He was making his way towards them from the other side of the common, a lead rope in one hand and a set of shears in the other.

'Going to teach Colin a bit of gardening?' Dylan teased as they got closer.

'Cheeky sod,' Fred said, although he didn't seem too bothered. 'Those bushes towards the river need trimming back, they might be poisonous.'

'Perhaps you shouldn't eat them, then,' was Dylan's swift reply.

'I mean for the horses, not me, as well you know.'

Misty looked anxiously from one face to the other but neither of them showed any sign of really meaning any of the insults they so casually slung to one another.

'So, what can I do you for?' Fred continued. 'Fancy helping? I need to get Colin fed, brushed and exercised after I've done some weeding.'

'Well, that's what we wanted to ask you about actually.' Dylan smoothly swayed the conversation back towards the matter at hand. 'You could do with some help, couldn't you?'

'Why, are you offering?' Fred looked sceptical at the possibility of Dylan volunteering to assist with anything.

'Not me,' Dylan replied hastily. 'Misty's dad. He's lost his job; he's sitting about all day moping—'

'That's not exactly what I said,' Misty interrupted before Dylan could say the wrong thing.

'But he needs something to do,' Dylan continued. 'So, I thought, perhaps you could do with an extra pair of hands?'

'I'm sure he'd be glad to help out,' Misty offered. 'He likes to keep busy. He likes to have... a project... to keep him occupied... I suppose.'

Fred looked doubtful for a second but to Misty's relief didn't start asking too many probing questions. Perhaps the hopeful look on her face had already told him everything that he needed to know.

'Leave it with me. I'll go up this afternoon and talk to your dad, see what I can do.'

Misty let out a huge breath that she hadn't realised she had been holding on to. Perhaps everything would turn out ok. Then all she'd have to worry about was how she was going to face ever going back to school again.

As Fred started to walk towards where Colin was tethered on the other side of the field, Dylan turned to Misty and asked, 'Well now that's all sorted, what do you want to do for the rest of the day? Shall we go to Merryford? We can take Sparkle with us this time. See what he makes of the seaside.'

Misty hadn't thought any further ahead than their plan to speak to Fred; she had been completely fixated on what they were going to say to him. As quickly as the lead weight across her shoulders had been lifted away it was replaced by an even heavier cloak of guilt when she thought of how she had deceived her father by taking another day off school. But that couldn't be helped, and perhaps once Fred had spoken to Dad, it would all be worth it. She decided to push away the uncomfortable feeling for now and concentrate on enjoying a day out with Dylan and the horses.

It took them slightly longer to reach the beach riding the two ponies bareback than it had taken in the cart, especially as they couldn't go very fast in case Misty lost her balance and fell onto the hard tarmac below. They trotted at a steady pace down the leafy country roads, Misty bobbing from side to side whilst working to stay upright on Sparkle's wide armchair-like back. It wasn't long before she settled, mesmerised by the sound of the even clip-clop of hoofbeats on the road and before she knew it, they were at the top of the road that led down to the beach, and she could see the stark glimmer of the waves in the late morning sun.

This time they didn't have to stop to dismantle the cart, and rode straight onto the sand, the ponies lifting their heads and snorting as the waves crashed onto the shore. Misty still felt a small twinge of pain just below her ribcage when she thought of her mum, but the beach seemed like a good place to remember her as she had been, happily camped out by the water, always with a book in hand, as she watched Misty build sandcastles and play in the sea.

'I'll race you!' Dylan shouted over the roar of the waves, pulling Misty back to the present, and without waiting for Misty's response he nudged Colin lightly in the side and they shot off together eager to be on the move.

Seeing the other pony go and anxious not to be left behind, Sparkle's slow trot became faster and faster as he tried to decrease the distance between himself and Colin, who was already making his way further across the small cove towards the other end of the shore. Misty's heart lurched as Sparkle accelerated sharply, and her breath caught in her throat as she was thrown unexpectedly forwards then backwards again as she struggled to stay onboard.

She grabbed hold of Sparkle's long, wavy mane in both hands and gripped her legs snugly around his warm hairy sides. When she discovered that she wasn't about to be thrown off, she let out a small laugh of surprise, and before she knew it, they had reached Dylan on the other side of the beach and Sparkle had slowed to a nice comfortable trot as he whinnied, happy to be reunited with Colin again.

'See, that wasn't so bad, was it?' Dylan grinned.

'You could have at least given me a bit more warning,' Misty said, trying her best to sound stern but smiling all the same. 'I could have been killed.'

'Don't be so dramatic. Even if you fell off, the sand's a soft enough landing. You just have to dust yourself down and get back on again.'

Misty had to admit that galloping across the beach was one of the most exhilarating things she had ever done. She patted Sparkle's solid neck as he pawed impatiently at the ground, ready to be off again.

'See, he's having great fun, let's go. Perhaps you can beat me this time.'

Misty spent the rest of the day racing Sparkle in a desperate attempt to try and beat Dylan. What Misty lacked in experience, Sparkle made up for in willingness, and his nimble body, when compared to Colin's lumbering carthorse physique, gave him an instant advantage. It wasn't long before Misty's confidence grew, and she was easily able to keep up with the other pair. They only stopped once the ponies began to tire, their breathing growing heavy, and as the sky darkened they knew that it was time to make their way back home.

When Misty arrived at the house, she was feeling much more optimistic than she had done when she had set out that morning. There was a pleasant glow coming from the kitchen and instead of dreading what she would find when she crossed its threshold, she bounced easily down the hallway and into the room. Her dad sat at the table as normal but this time there was no sign of any mess, and a pot of water was bubbling gently on the stove.

'Good day at school?' Dad asked as she sat down across from him.

Misty paused guiltily, as she tried to think of a convincing reply. 'Great—'

'How are Ruby and Jasmine getting on? Have you told them about the move yet? Why don't you invite them over this weekend? Now we're a bit more settled.'

Misty was relieved that her dad had stopped asking about school but unwittingly he had switched to an even trickier subject.

'I'll ask them tomorrow,' Misty said and promptly changed tack. 'What's for dinner?'

'I'm making a curry,' Dad announced. Thankfully, he didn't seem to have noticed the sudden shift in subject. 'Oh, one of our neighbours popped in earlier. Fred, Judy's brother-in-law.'

Misty's heart lifted. She tried her best not to sound too interested.

'Oh, right?'

'He asked if I wanted to help him with the allotments. He said with the horses and all the other jobs he does round the estate he doesn't have much time for them.'

'What did you say?' Misty asked, still attempting to sound nonchalant.

'I said I'd be happy to give it a go. I've got nothing better to do after all.' He let out a short laugh.

'That's good, perhaps he might need your help with some other repairs too. Once he gets to know you a bit better.'

'Perhaps.' Dad paused, lost in thought for a moment. 'At least it'll give me something to do during the day, whilst you're at school.'

Misty pushed away her discomfort for the second time that day. If her dad could start a new life here, she would need to do her bit and start keeping her promises too. Perhaps she could make up with Ruby and invite her best friends over. She could even show them the common and the horses, and introduce them to Dylan, and to Fred and Carin. Whatever happened, she was ready to face school with her head held high.

CHAPTER SIXTEEN

When Misty went back to school the next day, Ruby was still doing her best to avoid her, but Jasmine seemed determined not to take sides and had even agreed to come over to Misty's house in Redbridge for a sleepover that weekend. Even her dad seemed a bit brighter now he was helping Fred with odd jobs around the estate, and when Misty returned from the common for dinner, he was full of plans for the allotment, his eyes lighting up as they discussed the merits of broad beans and sugar snap peas.

Before Misty could blink, it was Friday and she was on the bus home with Jasmine, uneasy about showing her the bald patch of grass she had come to care so much for. She wondered what Jasmine would make of Dylan and Fred's mock fighting, Carin's mild tendency towards grumpiness and, most importantly, what she would think of Sparkle.

But Jasmine was keen to see the common and meet the people Misty had been telling her about. As if reading her mind, Jasmine's voice broke into the haze of Misty's thoughts, 'So, this Dylan, then?' she asked hesitantly. 'Is he your boyfriend?'

If Ruby had been here, she would have been piling on the questions until Misty was forced to react. But Jasmine's line of enquiry was much more subtle, and Misty found that she didn't mind so much.

'No, he's just my friend,' she answered honestly. 'We've gotten close but it's not a romantic thing.'

Instead of probing further as Ruby would've, Jasmine took Misty's words at face value.

'He's helped me a lot,' Misty continued. 'He's—' Misty stopped abruptly, finding it difficult to explain everything Dylan had done for her in the short time she had known him. 'He's a great friend,' she added simply.

Well, I can't wait to meet him,' Jasmine replied earnestly, seemingly satisfied with Misty's limited explanation. 'Look, we're nearly there.'

Jasmine was pointing at a large blue sign that marked the entrance to the estate. As Misty's eyes adjusted to the late afternoon gloom, she saw a solitary figure at the bus stop. It took her a moment to clock the mop of thick brown hair but then the figure began to wave, and she realised with a start that it was Dylan.

'Dylan?' Misty stuttered. 'What are you doing here?'

Surely, he couldn't have been so keen to meet Jasmine that he had decided to come straight there rather than going to the common as they had previously arranged. As if seeing her for the first time through Dylan's eyes, she noticed begrudgingly that Jasmine looked just like a model with her striking white hair and long, slender frame. She pushed the ungracious thought away and turned back to face Dylan.

'Is everything ok?' she asked.

By this time, Jasmine was looking back and forth between the pair uneasily, as if she sensed that something was wrong. Without saying a word or introducing himself to Jasmine, Dylan handed Misty a letter, the stark white pages glowing in the dimness. There was an official-looking letterhead at the top of it, and as Misty skimmed the words, she struggled to comprehend what they meant. When she reached the end of the letter, her heart sank to her knees.

'It's from the council,' explained Dylan. 'Fred knew those men he saw on the common were up to something.'

'It can't be true? Can it?' she muttered, still struggling to take it all in. 'They can't take the common away from us. Can they?'

'What does it say?' Jasmine asked. Misty gave her the letter wordlessly, still having difficulty making sense of it all. Jasmine quickly scanned the page. 'It says that the council want to sell the common, that it's going to be turned into luxury flats.'

'They can't do that, surely?' Dylan looked mystified. 'Fred said it was public land, didn't he?'

'I'm not sure,' Misty said slowly. Her mind was buzzing angrily as she tried to think of something useful to say. She had been so preoccupied with her fight with Ruby and aside from Fred, no one had believed that the threat from the council was a real possibility. She sifted through her thoughts, but it was like reading a book that wasn't making any sense, the pages becoming more muddled the harder she looked at them. Then, as if she had picked up a magnifying glass, her mind suddenly shifted into place.

'Jasmine, do you think your dad could help us?' she asked.

Jasmine's dad was a journalist at *The Herald*, one of the main newspapers in the city. He was a known 'social justice warrior', fighting fly-tipping and introducing a beach-cleaning initiative that now took place annually. Surely, he would know what could be done to save the common?

'I'm not sure,' Jasmine pondered. 'It's definitely worth a try. I can ask him when I get home tomorrow if you want?'

Dylan suddenly looked galvanised. 'Great. We should try and get everyone together. No one's taking our common away from us without a fight.'

'What we need is a massive publicity stunt, something that will get everyone talking about this place,' Jasmine suggested.

'Let's go find Fred,' Dylan replied. 'He might have some ideas.'

Their budding plan had energised the group, spurring them into action. They ran across the common and burst into the yard to find Fred and the others, wheezing heavily as they struggled to catch their breath. Fred was sitting on the steps of his caravan, a mug of coffee concealed within his sizeable hands. Carin was on the opposite side of the yard, brushing out Solo's long wiry tail and glanced up in surprise as they clattered to a halt on the concrete.

'You've seen it then?' Fred asked.

'Mum showed it to me when I got home,' Dylan said. 'What are we going to do?'

'What can we do?' Carin countered, a resigned expression on her face.

'This is Jasmine,' Misty said, introducing one of her oldest friends to her newest ones. 'Her dad works for *The Herald*. He might be able to help us.'

'Finally turned up then?' Carin muttered suspiciously. 'One of your fancy friends?'

'Carin,' Fred warned. 'Be nice.'

'Perhaps you could start a petition?' Jasmine suggested, tactfully ignoring Carin's previous remark. 'The newspaper could probably help with that.'

Carin continued to brush Solo's tail, looking doubtful,

but Dylan's eyes were lit with determination and even Fred was starting to look a bit more positive.

'We just need to come up with some ideas,' Misty said.

'I think we should go to the council office and confront them,' Carin countered defiantly. 'Tell them they can't have it. That it belongs to us.'

'I'm not sure it's that simple,' Misty replied. 'According to the letter they can.'

'I'll ask Mum if we can use the community centre for a meeting,' Dylan offered. 'Come on, let's go and find her.'

After Misty had quickly introduced Jasmine to Sparkle, they went with Dylan to find Judy, who was watching TV with Bethany. She looked up in surprise as a trio of teenagers crashed into the room.

'Mum,' Dylan gasped, not pausing to say hello. 'Can we use the hall at the community centre for a meeting? We want to get everyone that lives on the estate together and find a way to save the common.'

'I don't see why not,' Judy replied. 'It's a terrible business all this. Why don't the three of you make some posters and I'll put one on the noticeboard in the community centre for you? You can put them all round the estate as well.'

'That's a good idea,' Misty said. 'When should we have the meeting?'

'How about next weekend?' Jasmine suggested. 'It gives us plenty of time to put up posters and let people know, and I can ask Dad if he can come too.'

'Great idea,' Misty answered. 'Let's get started.'

Judy fetched an old biscuit tin which was jammed full of colourful pens and pencils and some large sheets of A3 paper that she had rescued from the recycling. Bethany asked if she could join in, so Dylan sat beside her at the dining table, and they started to decorate the edges of the posters with pictures of horses that she had cut out of old magazines.

'You don't have to do all this,' Misty said to Jasmine as they settled down on the living-room floor, pens at the ready.

'What do you mean?' Jasmine furrowed her brow in a familiar gesture that Misty knew meant that she was confused and wanted to avoid confrontation.

'This,' Misty gestured at the large sheets of coloured paper that were scattered at their feet, 'the common. Redbridge. None of it means anything to you.'

'But it means something to you.' Jasmine paused for a second to gather her thoughts. 'If it's important to you, then it's important to me.'

'What about Ruby?' Misty asked.

'What about Ruby? She'll come round. Her pride's just taken a bashing. You know how she likes to be at the centre of things, she's just hurt that she was left out of something for once.'

'Thanks, Jasmine.' Misty smiled weakly. She wasn't convinced that Ruby would ever forgive her, that they'd ever truly be friends again. 'I was so scared of what you would both think of Redbridge, I should have trusted you, I'm sorry.'

Jasmine wrapped her arm around Misty's shoulders and squeezed her tightly. 'You'll always be one of my best friends, wherever you live. Now come on, we've got posters to make.'

The three girls and Dylan spent the next couple of hours working on their colourful designs. Misty added a drawing of Sparkle to the bottom of every page using a silver gel pen and Jasmine used bright felt tips to write out the details of the meeting. By seven o'clock, Misty realised with a start that they had better get back for dinner as her dad would be wondering where on earth they were.

'What do you think of everyone?' Misty asked Jasmine as they struggled against the wind.

'Dylan seems nice,' Jasmine said diplomatically. 'And Sparkle is gorgeous.'

'Carin's all right too, once you get to know her,' Misty replied, sensing her friend's unease. 'She's very protective of Dylan, it's almost territorial.'

I'm glad you've made friends.' Jasmine smiled. 'I'm sorry you didn't think we would like it here.'

They had been so busy all evening that Misty hadn't even had time to reflect on how mortified she had been at the thought of bringing Jasmine to her new home. Now as they got closer, she realised that she shouldn't have been so bothered, Jasmine seemed to be taking everything in her stride as usual. She just wasn't convinced that Ruby would feel the same way.

After eating a hearty stew that Misty's dad had prepared for them, the two girls carried on discussing ideas for the meeting. They had explained to Misty's dad what had happened, and he was almost as outraged as they were, offering to help in any way he could. He even brought up hot chocolate and biscuits but, to Misty's surprise, he didn't tell them that they had to get to bed soon, he just left them to it, leaving the door slightly ajar as he made his way along the corridor to his own bedroom at the back of the house. Eventually, the girls' eyelids began to grow heavy. It was almost midnight, a new record for Jasmine, and they were both feeling very tired despite their best efforts to remain awake.

'I'll start putting the posters up in the morning,' Misty declared sleepily. 'One on every lamppost, the bus stop and the high street.'

'Sounds good.' Jasmine yawned and rubbed her eyes blearily. 'I'm sure Dylan will help.'

With the next phase of their plan decided, the girls fell fast asleep almost before their heads had touched their pillows. They were top-to-tail in Misty's single bed, which although keeping them warm, didn't make for the most comfortable night's sleep. Misty tossed and turned restlessly as she dreamt of Dylan and Sparkle and all the adventures they would continue to have together, as soon as the common was saved.

CHAPTER SEVENTEEN

Jasmine left early the next morning, after first promising Misty that she would speak to her dad as soon as she got home. At ten o'clock, Misty met Dylan outside the community centre, and they began putting up photocopies of their eye-catching posters everywhere they could think of. By lunchtime, they had covered almost every corner of Redbridge, plastering every available surface with news of the upcoming meeting.

'Do you think we should hand out flyers as well?' asked Dylan.

'I think that's a good idea. We can get Jasmine to help us after school this week.'

'And I can ask Mum to photocopy them for us. About one hundred copies should be enough.'

'Are you ok?' Misty asked. She couldn't help wondering how Dylan was still bursting with energy despite the threat to his home.

'I'm fine. I am worried about the common of course,' he replied. 'I've lived on this estate my entire life. I don't know what I'd do without the common and the horses. I won't let anyone take it from us.'

If Misty had felt committed to the cause before, she felt completely riled up now, she wanted nothing more than to save the common, not just for herself but for Sparkle and for Dylan too. Redbridge was her home now, and she had a responsibility to try and save it.

'Don't worry,' she tried to reassure him. 'Jasmine's dad will help us. We'll find a way to stop the council, whatever it takes.'

'Do you think a petition will be enough?' Dylan asked, looking thoughtful.

'It's a start I suppose, but I'm sure we'll think of some other ideas.'

'What about a protest?' Dylan suggested.

'A protest would be good, but it would need to be somewhere busy where lots of people would see it. Perhaps we could ask Jasmine's dad to help us with that too?'

On Monday morning, Misty met Jasmine in the playground before school. Jasmine had been busy training all weekend, so on Sunday evening, when Misty still hadn't heard anything, she had texted Jasmine to remind her to ask her dad about the common and whether he'd be willing to help them. As soon as she saw the familiar flash of blonde hair, she raced over to meet her.

'What did your dad say?' Misty blurted out as soon as she was within earshot.

'He said he'd love to help,' Jasmine replied soothingly, as she pushed her glasses up her nose. 'He'll come to the meeting on Saturday and put the details of the petition in the newspaper.'

'That's great news.' Misty let out a sigh of relief. 'Do you want to come to mine after school? We're going to make a flyer to hand out around town and we could do with coming up with some more ideas before the meeting. Dylan suggested a protest.'

'That could work,' ventured Jasmine. 'It would certainly get people's attention.'

'That's what I thought,' Misty confirmed. 'But it would need to be somewhere with lots of passersby, like in the centre of town somewhere.'

'A flashmob?' Jasmine suggested wistfully, thinking of how good Ruby would be at arranging something like that. Neither Jasmine nor Misty had heard anything from Ruby over the weekend and there was no sign of her in the playground that morning either.

As the girls continued to think about where they could hold a protest, the bell rang, and they walked to their form group together still throwing different ideas around as they went.

*

After school was finished for the day, Misty and Jasmine went back to Redbridge to meet Dylan. This time, Carin was also there waiting for them, and the group walked to Misty's house to start working on the flyers that they were going to hand out the next day. Just as they were settling onto the sofa in the living room, Jasmine's phone pinged and her face fell as she read the message that had appeared on the home screen, distorting the picture of the three friends she had set as her background.

'What is it?' Misty asked, a familiar plummeting sensation lodging in the depths of her stomach as she guessed who it was from.

'It's Ruby,' Jasmine said, confirming Misty's fear. 'It sounds like she's having a really hard time at the moment.'

Carin cocked her head to one side and Dylan looked down at the floor resolutely, doing his best not to get involved. Misty tried to fight the urge to ask what was wrong but eventually curiosity got the better of her.

'What do you mean?' she asked hesitantly.

'I'm sure it's nothing really. She's just been under a lot of pressure from her mum recently. After all the time she spent on the school play, Sheila's worried she's not concentrating hard enough on her studies. You know how strict she can be.'

Misty couldn't help feeling a little bit sorry for Ruby. Her mum was so driven and successful that sometimes

Ruby found it hard to live up to her high expectations. Ruby wanted, more than anything, to be an artist or a performer of some kind one day, but she was terrified of admitting this to her mum who thought that she was destined to become a doctor, a businesswoman, or a lawyer like her.

'I've been wondering if that's partly why she's been acting up recently,' Jasmine continued. 'I think she's fed up with trying to please her mum all the time.'

'Even so, she shouldn't have taken it out on me,' Misty replied. But she knew deep down she could hardly take the moral high ground when she had been just as much in the wrong as Ruby, lying to her best friends for so long.

'Perhaps I'll try and speak to her,' Misty resolved.

'What do you think of this?' Dylan asked the girls, once they had finished their conversation. He was holding up his design for the flyer, on one side he had written *SAVE OUR COMMON* in bold, bright lettering and on the other he had included all the details for the upcoming meeting.

'It looks brilliant,' Misty said. 'Have you had any more thoughts about the protest?'

'I think it's a good idea,' Carin interjected. 'Shows them we're serious.'

'And we can get my dad to publicise it,' Jasmine offered. 'Let's see if anyone else has any suggestions at the meeting on Saturday.'

'Thanks, Jasmine,' Dylan replied and even Carin, who raised her head and smiled, seemed to have started to thaw.

'We really appreciate everything you're doing to help us,' Misty told Jasmine sincerely. 'Hopefully lots of people will come to the meeting and the protest if we organise it well.'

On Tuesday morning, inspired by her conversation with Jasmine, Misty went to find Ruby. She was hoping they would be able to mend the tear in their friendship. She thought that if she apologised for concealing the truth from her, Ruby would in turn admit that she had also been in the wrong. However, when she got to the school playground, there was no sign of Ruby anywhere and when she asked Jasmine, she hadn't seen her either.

'But where can she be?' Misty asked Jasmine at lunchtime, when she still hadn't managed to track Ruby down. 'There can't be that many places to hide in this school.'

'Maybe she doesn't want to be found,' Jasmine conceded. 'Maybe she needs more time.'

They had searched the hallways, peering into empty classrooms and getting told off for not being outside in the fresh air. They had looked in the girls' toilets on every floor and in the school hall where the drama club usually took place. They had even searched the football fields, but of course, there was no sign of her there.

'Maybe,' Misty admitted, feeling somewhat frustrated that her plan to make up with Ruby had already failed.

'Just give her time,' Jasmine advised. 'She'll come round in the end.'

As she walked to her afternoon lessons, Misty hoped that Jasmine was right. She couldn't help being angry with Ruby, not just for the way she had reacted when she had found out about Redbridge but for how stubborn she had been since then. Surely, Ruby could see that Misty hadn't wanted any of this to happen. That she needed her friends now more than ever. If Ruby couldn't see that, perhaps they were better off not being friends at all.

After school that day, Misty tried not to dwell on the situation with Ruby, as she had arranged to meet Dylan on the high street to hand out their newly created flyers. To Misty's surprise, most people they approached were more than willing to take a leaflet and to chat about what was happening on the estate and what could be done to stop it.

The more people they talked to, the more passionate Misty became, as they discussed how important it was to save the common for good. By the time she got home that evening, she was coiled with excitement, sure that their plans would work. She found her dad in the backyard, working on the garden he was creating to brighten up the small, empty space. With Judy's help, they had salvaged a variety of recycled containers to fill with wildflowers they had found in the hedgerows around the estate.

'This looks great, Dad,' Misty called as she looked out from beside the back door.

'Thanks, love.' Dad paused to wipe a stray bit of dirt from his brow.

As Misty had watched the yard transform from a dismal concrete square to a joyful and tranquil space, she had noticed her dad's mood also seemed to have lightened. He was enjoying making new friends and helping people with Fred. He seemed much more settled in Redbridge now, as if the fresh start he had promised them both was starting to do him some good. She just hoped he would never find out about the final day of school she had missed in order to help them achieve it.

'How was town?' he asked. 'Did you hand out many flyers?'

'All of them,' Misty replied happily. 'I think a lot of people will come along to support us.'

'I'm sure they will,' Dad replied as he dusted himself off and walked back into the house. 'I'm glad to see you and Jasmine are thick as thieves again.'

Misty gave a small smile in acknowledgement, if only he knew how desperate she was to see Ruby and be reunited with her too.

CHAPTER EIGHTEEN

The day of the meeting dawned bright and clear. At half eleven, both Misty and Jasmine were outside the front door ready for Jasmine's dad to arrive, having been up since the crack of dawn. They had agreed to meet Dylan at the community centre at a quarter to twelve, just before the gathering was due to begin.

'What if no one turns up?' Misty ventured nervously. 'This could be a total waste of time.'

'I'm sure that's not going to happen,' Jasmine replied firmly. 'I've only been coming here for a short time and even I can see how important the common is to everyone who lives here.'

Before Misty could answer, they heard the rev of a car engine as it struggled up the hill towards them. Then Clive appeared in his beloved clapped-out Ford Capri, waving cheerfully as the car groaned and stuttered to a clanking halt.

'All ready?' he asked amicably as he jostled with the car door.

When he finally opened the door, which gave a deafening shriek of protest, he made his way languidly towards them. Clive didn't appear to be paying the slightest bit of attention to the unfamiliarity of his new surroundings, and was taking that part at least in his long, lanky stride, just as his daughter had previously.

'Thank you for agreeing to help us,' Misty said breathlessly, anxious to be on their way.

They were just about to leave, when they heard the click of the latch behind them, and Misty's dad appeared on the stoop. He had thrown on an old, oversized denim jacket and his work boots and looked as if he was about to spend the day with Fred down at the allotments.

'OK, let's go,' Misty jumped in. 'Dylan will be waiting for us.'

'Lead on, fair maidens,' Clive replied with a somewhat dramatic flourish of his arms. He was just as bizarre, if not more so, than Jasmine's mum, Ivy.

Misty swiftly rearranged her face into a less whimsical expression and took her dad's arm in her own. She hadn't been certain that he would want to come with them, and she felt guilty that she had doubted him. She took a deep breath, and they marched down the hill together, two by two, until they arrived at the squat red-brick building that marked the central hub of the local community.

*

Dylan and the rest of his family were already outside; Judy stood beside him, with Bethany and Carin and Fred behind them. Misty realised that she was surrounded by the people she loved most and that feeling buoyed her on. Only Ruby was missing, Misty thought miserably, as she introduced them all to Clive before everyone filed inside. They made a strange ensemble, but everyone seemed to be getting on fine, more than fine in fact.

Misty breathed out a heavy sigh of relief when she saw the group of people scattered throughout the hall. It wasn't exactly hundreds of people but at least some of their neighbours had turned up. They watched expectantly from their foldout chairs as Misty and her peculiar entourage entered the room.

Misty had been so focused on organising the meeting, she hadn't thought about what would happen next. *What on earth are we going to say?* A stagnant hush filled the air as every set of eyes in the room seemed to burn into Misty's back as she made her way to a seat at the front of the room. Luckily, just as Misty was starting to wonder if they'd made a mistake, Fred jumped in.

'This is Clive,' he started, pointing a short stubby finger in the direction of Jasmine's dad. 'He's from the local paper. He thinks he might be able to help us save the common.'

An old lady at the back of the room coughed loudly

but otherwise nobody said a word. All eyes were on Fred as he made his unlikely speech.

'But if we *are* going to save it, we need everyone's help. Not just Clive's. He doesn't even live here for a start, but we do.' Fred's voice gained strength as he continued. He might not have been the most obvious or eloquent spokesperson, but he was passionate about his home and the people and horses who lived within it. By the time he had finished talking, his voice had risen to a fervent boom. 'We need a plan. Something that will get everybody's attention. The press, the council's, everyone's.'

'I thought we could stage a protest,' said Dylan. 'And we could start a petition and get everyone to sign it.'

'Whatever we do, it needs to be memorable,' Misty explained. 'And somewhere where lots of people will see it.'

'What about a procession?' Carin said suddenly, her eyes lighting up eagerly as she spoke. 'Through the city centre. With the horses and carts. Hold up the traffic. Everyone will have to listen to what we've got to say then.'

There were faint mutters and nods of approval from those dotted around the room.

'The horses should definitely be involved,' someone shouted out. 'It's their home too.'

Misty felt a bubble of anticipation emerge from the bottom of her belly. It fizzed and popped as she thought of riding Sparkle through the lively streets of the city centre.

'We should have it on a weekend,' she said firmly. 'We need to act quickly, and more people will be in town then, so we're bound to get more attention.'

It felt as though thousands of pairs of eyes turned to look at her as she spoke, when in fact there were only around thirty or forty people in the room. For a second Misty wondered what they would think of a relative outsider making suggestions on their behalf, but she saw no judgement on the curious faces that were now pointing towards her. Only a slight wariness as people weighed up the possible outcomes of stopping traffic in the centre of town on a busy Saturday morning.

'Well, I think it's a great idea,' Dylan said, coming to her rescue when no one else spoke.

Clive, who had been silently scribbling notes in an old exercise book, suddenly piped up, 'You'll need a permit.'

When a sea of blank faces looked back at him, he continued, 'For the parade. From the council.'

Misty felt the bubble in her belly burst as she thought about how long it might take to organise a permit.

As if he had read her mind, Dylan said, 'It'll take too long. We don't have time to sit around all day waiting for the council to make up their minds. When have we ever needed a piece of paper to tell us what to do?' He grinned fiendishly.

'Well, don't say I didn't warn you,' replied Clive, though he was smiling as he said it. 'I'll put the petition in the paper on Friday. Hopefully lots of people will sign it.'

And just like that it was decided. They had a plan to try and save the common. After the meeting, Jasmine went home with her dad, and Misty and Dylan spent the rest of the weekend with the horses, planning every aspect of the procession with a surgeon's precision. No stone was left unturned as they discussed who would take part, what the horses and riders could wear and whether they should paint signs for the carts. One thing was certain, it was going to be a very busy time in the lead up to the parade.

On Thursday evening, Misty went round to Jasmine's house after school, where Clive was putting together the notice that was going to be in the newspaper the following day. They had decided that the parade would take place on the first day of the May half-term holiday, which was now only three weeks away and they still had a lot to prepare. They hoped that on that day the high street would be packed with shoppers, who would have no choice but to stop and watch the passing parade which they were planning to take straight through the centre of town.

Misty had hoped that she might be able to make up with Ruby and get her involved, but Ruby still seemed to be doing her best to avoid both her and Jasmine, as if she was equally annoyed at them both. They had discovered that she spent most of her lunchbreaks studying in the school library, head buried deeply in a textbook, surrounded by mounds of scribbled-on and crossed-out papers. If Misty hadn't had so many other things on her mind, she would have found Ruby's behaviour deeply troubling; it was as if she'd had a personality transplant and been replaced with a new, subdued version of Ruby, one that was only a shadow of her former bubbly self.

'Are you worried about Ruby?' Misty asked Jasmine as they made their way through Jasmine's front gate and into her unruly garden. They were surrounded by a glut of budding spring flowers, a riot of vibrant colour that burst out from deep-green stems in every direction. 'I know you said I needed to give her time but this—'

'A bit,' Jasmine admitted. 'It isn't like her to hold onto a grudge for this long. And she is behaving totally out of character.'

Misty nodded in agreement. Ruby was fiery, letting out her anger like a flamethrower before she simmered down and all was usually forgotten before too long. Misty's own anger had been replaced with an empty hollow feeling when she thought about life without her best friend. However, as soon as Jasmine opened the front door and Teddy bounded out to greet them, Ruby's predicament was temporarily forgotten as the two girls darted up the stairs to find Clive in his office at the back of the house.

'Hi Dad,' Jasmine panted, slightly out of breath from their run. 'How's it going?'

Teddy was barking excitedly, jumping up at the two girls and racing in concentric circles around their feet despite the confines of the tightly packed room. The walls were lined with shelves of back-dated newspapers and fusty hardback books, with just enough space for a desk and a chair which were crammed under the window at the other end of the room.

'I'm almost done,' Clive replied.

He turned so that the girls could see the document that was open on his computer screen and Misty quickly scanned its contents.

'*Petition to save Redbridge Common*,' she read aloud. Underneath the headline, Clive had spelled out the council's plans to turn the common into flats and included a link to sign the petition which would go live on *The Herald*'s website the following morning.

'I'll put in the date of the parade nearer to the time,' Clive explained. 'We don't want the council getting wind and trying to put a stop to it if we put it in too early.'

'What if no one from the council turns up?' Jasmine asked.

'Don't you worry, they'll definitely want to be there once they find out what's happening. I'll call the councillor myself to make sure of it.'

'This is perfect, thank you.' Misty beamed at him. 'We can present the petition to the council at the end of the parade.'

The parade would finish in front of the council offices at the bottom of the high street and Misty and Dylan had asked Fred if he would present the signed document to the local councillor when they got there. Everything was starting to fall into place and Misty felt their plan burst alight, warming her from the inside out. They still had the signs and banners to design, and the route to formalise, but with only a short time left to go, she was beginning to feel confident that everything would be organised on time.

'Dinner's ready,' Ivy shouted from the landing at the bottom of the stairs. 'It's radish and spinach pie.'

Misty let out a surprised giggle and even Clive looked slightly alarmed.

'We'd better go down,' Jasmine said, bracing herself for her mum's latest culinary invention.

'I'm sure it'll be delicious,' Misty said graciously though she was still struggling to contain her laughter.

'Mmm, radishes!' Jasmine replied, rolling her eyes. 'At least we can give Ted any leftovers, he'll eat anything.'

The girls followed Clive as he made his way into the dining room. Teddy was as enthusiastic about Ivy's cooking as ever and he made a beeline for the kitchen, nose thrust in the air as he went.

'That's not for you,' they heard Ivy admonish from the kitchen. She appeared a few moments later, pie dish in hand, with Teddy staring up at her in adoration as she set it down in the centre of the table.

'Dig in,' Ivy said, turning to Misty. 'Jasmine's been telling me all about what's been happening in Redbridge, we'll do whatever we can to support you.'

'Thanks, Ivy,' Misty replied, as she ladled a steaming portion of pie onto her plate. 'I think we've got it all under control.'

'Well, let me know if you need anything at all. Catering? Perhaps Teddy could be your mascot?'

'This is amazing, Mum,' Jasmine interrupted gesturing towards her meal and rescuing Misty from having to think of a feeble excuse. The last thing they needed was an unruly Teddy ruining the parade and she wasn't sure if the people of Redbridge were quite ready for quinoa and mung beans quite yet – she wasn't sure anyone was.

CHAPTER NINETEEN

Before long it was the final week of the half term. Ruby was so caught up in her studies that Misty couldn't have spent any time with her even if she had wanted to. And every spare moment Misty had was taken up with preparations for the parade the following weekend. Her evenings were consumed with getting the horses and ponies that lived on the common ready for their big day. Her dad, Fred and Judy were also doing everything they could to help out.

So Misty was amazed when she got back to Redbridge on the final day before the spring break and found someone with a familiar head of wild dark curls waiting for her at the bottom of the hill.

'Ruby!' she exclaimed in surprise. As Misty's brain adjusted to the shock of seeing her friend there, Misty noticed tears glistening in the corners of Ruby's large deer-like brown eyes. 'What are you doing here? What's wrong?'

'I didn't know where else to go.' Ruby stared dejectedly at the floor. 'I *had* nowhere else to go.' She continued to eye the pavements of Redbridge suspiciously, as if they had done something to personally offend her. 'I know you're annoyed with me.' She kicked sheepishly at a loose stone with the corner of her trainer.

Misty knew a Ruby-shaped peace offering when she saw one, but she also knew that Ruby wasn't just here to make up with her. Something must have happened for her to come to Redbridge like this. She checked her phone; it was almost four thirty and she had promised to meet Dylan soon. They still had some final preparations to make for the parade.

'I have to go,' Misty said slowly. 'I've arranged to meet someone... a friend. I'm already late.'

A familiar look of annoyance rose to Ruby's face, but it was replaced with a look of overwhelming sadness, making her whole body tremble. 'But I've come all this way... here,' Ruby looked around her in distaste and gestured towards the estate that rose up the hill in front of them. 'You *have* to listen to me.'

Misty could see that nothing had changed. Ruby's obvious disapproval of her surroundings and her sense of entitlement made Misty quiver with anger. Her hands were shaking with nerves as she struggled to put her feelings into words that would be comprehensible to her friend.

'I don't,' she began finally. 'I'm sorry I lied to you, but I don't *owe* you anything. I have to help my friends *here*.

In this place that seems to offend you so greatly. They have *real* problems. Problems you would know about if you had taken the time to care.'

'I *do* care,' Ruby blurted out, seemingly having a change of heart. 'I'm sorry I haven't been there for you. I've had so much going on with my mum. She's putting so much pressure on me to do well at school. And now she's said that I can't go to the school disco unless my marks improve. I guess I was jealous that you had this new life and new friends and seemed to be getting on just fine without me.'

'But it wasn't like that at all,' Misty exclaimed. 'I didn't want to come here. I didn't want a new life or new friends, and I certainly didn't want to lose my old ones. That's why I didn't tell you. And look what happened when you found out. Exactly what I was afraid of.'

There was a moment of silence. Then Misty began explaining to Ruby about the parade they had planned, about the newspaper coverage that Clive had organised, about the council threatening to sell the common, about Dylan and the horses. Sparkle even. Before she could stop, the events of the past few months spilled out of her like a river in full flow. The dam she had built in her mind opened and her story poured out.

Ruby's face began to crumble, and Misty exhaled. 'If you want to be friends again,' Misty offered, 'you have to understand that *this* is my home now and the people who live here mean a lot to me. I'm sorry you've been having a hard time, I really am, and I want to help, but I need you to want to help me too.'

With that final remark, Misty walked away and left her friend standing alone by the roadside, a significant part of her hoping that Ruby would call after her and tell her not to go.

When Misty arrived at the common, shoulders hunched towards her ears, Dylan noticed straightaway that something wasn't right.

'What's up?'

'Nothing. I'm fine,' Misty replied though her face was downcast. 'What do we need to do now?'

Much to Misty's relief, Dylan took one look at her face and decided not to push any further. She knew her brow was set in a line of stubborn, single-minded concentration, and she would tell him what was bothering her as soon as she was able.

'Fred's just adding the finished banners to the carts. I said we'd meet everyone down at the yard.'

'OK,' Misty said, still feeling preoccupied as they trudged silently across the field. As she walked, the regular beat of her own footsteps caused her thudding heart to fall into pace. By the time they had reached Fred's, Misty was feeling a bit more like her old self again. With or without

Ruby, she needed to focus all her energy on the parade tomorrow and making the council listen to them.

The drab concrete yard had been transformed into a display of rebellion. The painted carts were hung with bright banners that shouted jubilantly. '*COMMON LAND FOR COMMON PEOPLE*,' called one. '*OUR HOME ISN'T FOR SALE*,' stated another. '*YOU CAN'T PUT A PRICE ON COMMON-ITY*,' was Misty's particular favourite.

'Wow,' Misty said breathlessly. 'This looks amazing.'

Fred beamed as he cast admiring glances over his handi-work. Carin and Bethany were polishing saddles and bridles until they gleamed spectacularly. Judy appeared from the caravan with two mugs of tea in her hands.

'I think we're almost ready,' she said as she handed one over to Fred. 'Not long to go now.'

Misty's mind swam fretfully. Would the council listen to them? Or would they be arrested for disturbing the peace? Holding an illegal protest in the centre of town on one of the busiest days of the week?

'Clive will meet us by the statue at the top of the high street at 10am promptly,' Fred explained. 'All we need to do is get the horses ready in the morning. Make sure Sparkle is absolutely sparkling.' He let out a booming laugh.

Judy had gone back to the caravan to get tea for the others and Misty was grateful to be holding a comforting drink in her hands. She took a long gulp and sighed as the warm liquid started its silent journey towards her stomach.

'Penguin?' Dylan offered, interrupting her thoughts.

Misty took the biscuit and bit into it greedily. Her stomach growled and she realised that she was ravenous, a biscuit wasn't going to cut it. She said her goodbyes and started to make her way towards the house where dinner would hopefully be waiting for her.

When Misty unlocked the front door, she could see light emanating from the kitchen and the reassuring smell of home cooking filled her nostrils. Unfashionable '80s rock music was playing loudly as Misty struggled out of her coat and made her way to the back of the house.

'In here, Misty,' her dad called without looking up from the pot he was stirring. 'Dinner's almost ready. All set for the big day?'

'I think so,' Misty replied eagerly as she stuck her head round the doorway.

'I'm looking forward to watching you all.'

Misty's dad smiled proudly as he ladled spoonfuls of steaming liquid into large round bowls. Misty couldn't remember when she had last seen him look so happy. His work with Fred on the allotments seemed to have transformed him.

'You are coming?' Misty asked.

'Wouldn't miss it for the world. Now eat up, before it gets cold. You'll need all the fuel you can get for tomorrow.'

They continued to eat their meal in contented silence. Dad had turned down the radio and they could hear a faint murmur in the background. Misty's butterflies had almost settled in the calm and relaxed atmosphere of her home.

Once they had finished their last few mouthfuls, Misty's dad spoke again.

'I've got something else to tell you,' he began. 'Some big news actually.'

Misty felt a hard lump forming in her throat, the rich casserole was suddenly much harder to digest. 'What is it?'

'Don't give me that look. It's good news, don't worry.'

'Yes?'

'I've got an interview next week. For a job at the local secondary school. Financial officer. So don't get into too much trouble at the parade.' He winked at her to show he was only joking.

'But that's great news, Dad,' Misty exclaimed. 'I knew you could do it!'

'It's a bit early for celebrations yet, but with all my experience—'

'I'm sure you'll get it, Dad. I'll keep my fingers crossed for you.' Misty crossed her middle and index fingers and held them up in an enthusiastic gesture of solidarity.

'I almost didn't tell you. I didn't want to get your hopes up, in case—'

'In case what, Dad? Everything's going to be ok,' Misty confirmed optimistically.

'If you say so.' Dad seemed to hesitate before continuing. 'I know I don't say it much, but I am proud of you. How you've handled moving here, adjusted, made new friends, and settled in so well.'

'I've had my moments,' Misty replied, thinking of the time she had spent bunking off school.

'Haven't we all.'

They burst out laughing. It was true they had both had their fair share of problems recently, but it seemed spring had arrived, and the buds of possibility were unfurling before them, offering them a new beginning.

'Right, shouldn't you be getting to bed?' Dad asked. 'Have an early night. You've got to be up at the crack of dawn.'

'Love you, Dad.' Misty wrapped her arm around her father's solid middle and huddled beneath his shoulder for a moment. 'See you in the morning.'

'Goodnight, pet.'

Misty was still grinning like a Cheshire cat as she changed into her pyjamas and got into bed. Jasmine had texted wishing her good luck for the next day but there was no message from Ruby. Misty felt a small twinge of guilt as she wondered if she had made it home ok. As she turned off the light and snuggled deeper under the covers, she pondered if she was ever going to make up with her other best friend again.

CHAPTER TWENTY

Misty groomed Sparkle until every inch of him gleamed; his shiny grey coat a reflection of the purple-tinged clouds above. Now, she glanced uneasily at the ominous sky and hoped it wasn't a warning for how the day was going to unfold.

'Ready?' Dylan asked. He would be riding in Colin's cart with Fred at the front of the group, followed by Misty on Sparkle and Carin on Solo, and Bethany with Buttons. The rest of the estate would follow behind; some riding bareback, some in an eclectic array of horse-drawn vehicles, and others on foot.

'I suppose.'

There were around fifty people and twenty horses and ponies in total and once they were all lined up ready to leave, the noise was deafening. Horses jangled their bridles and snorted, impatient to be on their way, people called out greetings over the heads of one another, and the wheels of rusty wagons squeaked angrily as they were forced into action.

'Right,' Fred shouted over the noise of the gathered crowd. 'Let's go. It's time to show the council who's boss round here.'

The group cheered loudly, and the horses tossed their heads, sensing the abrupt change in the atmosphere. The air above them was charged with an invisible electric current. They surged forwards and started to follow Fred, Dylan and Colin as they made their way out of the yard and onto the road that eventually led to the centre of the city. Colin's feathers had been scrubbed bright-white and offered a beacon of sunshine for the others to follow as his hooves tapped out a merry rhythm on the street in front of him.

Misty looked round eagerly for her father and spotted him waving from his place at the back of the group. He was walking alongside Judy, and another woman who Misty hadn't seen before. They all seemed to be chatting away agreeably about something. As arranged, the group would be joined by Jasmine and Clive once they reached their destination. Misty settled in for the half-hour ride and gave Sparkle what she hoped was a reassuring pat on his neck. He snickered softly, responsive as ever to her touch, and she knew that whatever happened today, Sparkle would always take care of her, no matter what.

*

As they made their way towards the tall grey cenotaph that dominated the bottom of the high street, Misty could see that Jasmine and Clive were already waiting for them, as promised. They didn't look very happy however, and on second glance, Misty realised that there was another figure beside them, an imposingly tall man who was wearing a smart suit and had a pointy white moustache.

As the ragtag band came closer to the serious-looking man and Misty's friends, more and more people were stopping in their tracks as they noticed the unusual sight of twenty horses and ponies coming towards them on a busy Saturday morning. Cars were forced to U-turn and retrace their steps as the procession halted the ongoing vehicles in their tracks.

'Look, Mummy,' shouted a red-faced toddler as he dragged a harassed-looking woman closer to the approaching procession.

When they reached the statue, Misty could see that Clive and the man in the suit were arguing animatedly. The man's moustache rose in agitation as he spoke, giving him the appearance of a comic-book villain.

'That must be the man from the council,' Dylan called out behind him. 'The one that wants to sell off the common to the highest bidder.'

Clive's phone call had obviously worked. The councillor was pulling angrily at his tie and gesturing towards the encroaching herd. When Fred's cart stopped beside the monument, the man raised his hand in warning.

'You're to go no further,' he shouted, his moustache twitching with displeasure. He looked down at a large silver watch on his wrist. 'You haven't got a permit. The police will be here in a minute.'

'*Police?*' Misty gasped.

Suddenly there was a commotion in the large mob that had gathered on the pavement beside them. A familiar face with a mass of curls was fighting her way through the crowd towards where Misty and Sparkle were standing. Pensioners were swiftly cast aside as she pushed her way forwards.

'Permit or no permit, I believe they should have a right to peacefully protest,' she yelled as she finally broke through the ocean of bodies. She pointed her finger indignantly at the councillor's face. 'And *you* can't do anything to stop them.'

'She's right.' Ruby's mum, Sheila, appeared behind her wearing her chicest outfit and gave the councillor her strongest glare.

'Ruby,' Jasmine cried as she hugged her. 'You came.'

Misty was struggling to see what was happening over the heads of the crowd, but she knew that adamant voice anywhere. She couldn't believe that Ruby had come, and it sounded like she was determined to get her own way. She had gently cast-off Jasmine's embrace and was eyeing the councillor defiantly, a mirror-image of her mother, daring him to object. For a second, neither the councillor nor Ruby and Sheila seemed willing to back down and were having a silent stand-off, like a scene from one of Misty's dad's old western films.

'You're not authorised to be here,' the councillor complained but everyone could see that his anger was deflating like an ageing balloon.

'It doesn't matter,' Sheila replied, giving him another defiant stare.

The weight of the gathered protesters seemed to press heavily against the councillor's back and after another moment where nobody seemed to breathe and still there was no sign of the police, he took a step backwards, and with his moustache drooping defeatedly, he held up the palms of his hands in surrender.

'Fine,' he snarled. 'But don't think for one second that your tiny parade is going to change anything. It's already been agreed. Those flats are going to be built one way or another.'

'Over my dead body,' Fred muttered under his breath as he flicked the reins that ran like train tracks along Colin's broad back. 'Right, everybody. Let's be off. We'll see you at the other end.'

By now all of the Saturday shoppers had stopped to see what all the fuss was about. A camera crew from the local news had arrived and were busy talking to Clive who had been furiously jotting down notes the whole time. Jasmine and Ruby clasped hands and made their way over to join the parade. The protestors took up their cries and marched purposefully down the centre of the high street; children on buses that had ground to a halt staring out of the windows, their breath steaming 'o's of surprise.

Before Misty could ask Ruby what she was doing here, she heard a shout. At first, she assumed it was part of the protest but then a timid-looking boy appeared on the crowded pavement in front of her. His neat, close-cropped blonde hair was flashing like a Belisha beacon as it moved towards her.

Although he wasn't very tall, Misty could tell that the boy was a similar age to her. With one last flash of his familiar straw-like hair, he was beside her, tugging Sparkle by the reins and forcing them both to a standstill. The pony struggled to keep his balance and turned at a right angle towards where the boy was standing. But before she had a moment to process where she had seen him before, the boy spoke.

'Give him back,' the boy commanded. 'That's my pony. That's my Silver.'

As Misty struggled to comprehend what on earth had just happened, the poor pony who now had two different names to contend with, let out a warm snicker of recognition and rubbed his bony head tenderly against the boy's shoulder, leaving Misty with no doubt that what he was saying was true.

CHAPTER TWENTY-ONE

'What?' Misty spluttered, though she knew that Sparkle didn't truly belong to her however much she wished that might be.

A stunned silence followed as neither party was willing to back down. Horses and carts rushed past, their riders throwing enquiring glances at the girl and her pony who had suddenly crashed to a halt. Misty could hear nothing except for a strange whooshing noise in her ears as she struggled to make sense of what had just happened.

'Get your hands off her,' came a familiar shout from the crowd as Ruby and Jasmine pushed their way towards her. The boy lowered his hands fearfully, but he didn't move an inch. By now Ruby and Jasmine had reached the silent stand-off that was taking place and they knew the instant they saw Misty's face that something terrible had occurred.

'Misty, what's wrong?' Jasmine asked.

'And who the hell are you?' Ruby glared at the stranger.

'That's my pony,' the boy continued desperately, gesturing towards Sparkle who tossed his head in agreement. 'He was stolen a few months ago. *She* must have taken him.'

'So, now you're calling our best friend a thief?' Ruby growled when Misty didn't reply.

'I'm sure there's been some misunderstanding,' Jasmine blurted out before an argument could ensue. 'Misty would never have stolen your pony.'

'I've been looking after him,' Misty said finally. 'He was found on the common in Redbridge, he was dumped there.'

'If he *is* your pony,' ventured Ruby. 'And that's a very BIG if, why would someone steal him from you and then just leave him like that? Why didn't they sell him? This doesn't make any sense.'

The boy's shoulders slumped miserably. Then he raised his head, and his eyes were glimmering with purpose. 'I'll prove it,' he said flatly. 'Don't worry, I'll be back.'

With that parting shot, he ran back through the crowd and the girls lost sight of him as he disappeared up a side street. Misty shuddered and let out a deep breath. She could tell from the way Sparkle's eyes had never left the boy that they were part of each other's lives. As she watched him retreat, Misty suddenly realised where she had seen the boy before.

'Well, I doubt we'll be seeing him again,' remarked Ruby. 'He's probably all talk and no trousers.'

'Do you think he's telling the truth?' Jasmine asked tentatively when she saw the look of dismay on Misty's face.

'I don't know,' Misty answered honestly. 'No one knows where Sparkle came from. He just turned up one day. It's a mystery.'

'For all we know that boy's lying, and he just wants a free pony,' Ruby countered.

'I don't think he's making it up,' Misty admitted miserably. 'I'm sure I saw him out riding on Sparkle when I first moved to Redbridge.'

'That still doesn't prove anything,' Ruby said. 'Maybe he just saw you with Sparkle and he thought he'd try his luck.'

'Dylan warned me that something like this might happen. That his real owner might turn up sooner or later,' Misty remarked, glad to have Ruby back on her team. 'I was too stubborn to take it seriously.'

By now they were right at the back of the parade, behind the stragglers who were still strolling slowly along the high street. Misty wanted to believe Ruby, who had just saved her skin for the second time that day, but she had seen the desperate look in the boy's eyes and knew that wouldn't be the last they would see of him.

'Let's catch up with the others,' Jasmine suggested, breaking the silence. 'We can tell them what happened. They might know what to do.'

The girls started walking briskly as they tried to catch up with the rest of the parade. Misty was still riding Sparkle, with Ruby on one side and Jasmine on the other, forming a protective barrier around her. Misty was so grateful to have them both with her at last. Without having to spell it out to her, Ruby's presence showed Misty that she was willing to put aside her misconceptions about Redbridge and get involved in the parade. Misty tried to convince herself that she would feel much better once she had spoken to Fred and Dylan, and they would reassure her that something could be done and Sparkle would be able to stay on the common.

As they approached the shopping precinct at the other end of the high street, Misty could see that the protestors and shoppers had formed a large disorderly cluster on the concrete paving stones in front of it. There was also another camera crew, and several reporters had congregated to cover the parade. Misty spotted Dylan at the top of the stairs that led into the large building, talking animatedly to a squirrelly-looking woman who was poised with a notebook and pen in hand, and he was grinning triumphantly as he spoke.

Misty waved briefly and tried to take in the success of the day. Apart from her own run-in with the strange boy, the parade had gone exactly to plan. She wanted to feel pleased but all she could think about was the bizarre conversation that had just taken place and what it meant for Sparkle.

Will he really be taken away? And if he is, will I ever be able to see him again? she wondered.

'That's her,' Dylan said proudly as she approached. 'That's Misty. This was her idea too.'

Misty smiled weakly. She could hardly explain to Dylan what had just happened when he was busy telling a reporter about the importance of the parade. With difficulty, she swallowed back the words that were forming in her throat and tried to focus her attention on what the woman in front of them was saying.

'So, you also live on the estate?' the reporter asked, tucking a strand of unruly dark hair behind her ear as she spoke.

'Yes,' Misty replied. 'It's my home. The common is my home. These are *my* friends and we're all here to make sure the council know we won't back down without a fight.'

Sparkle neighed in agreement, he seemed to have already forgotten seeing the mystery boy who could be his real owner. The reporter laughed and held out her palm for Sparkle to sniff.

'He's a lovely pony,' she said fondly. 'I used to ride too when I was your age.'

A pair of strong arms wrapped Misty in a hug, and she was rescued from having to think of a reply that wouldn't upset her. 'There you are, love,' her dad said. 'I've been looking everywhere for you. Jasmine said you were around here somewhere.'

Suddenly, all Misty wanted was to be at home, in the house at Redbridge, sitting beside her dad in the kitchen with a warm cup of tea in front of her, but she knew they had to stay and put up their best fight. So instead, she smiled weakly at her dad and let him continue to hold her in a comforting embrace.

Once everyone had gathered on the steps of the council building, they spread out to form a pathway for Fred, who took his place at the head of the group clutching a copy of the petition in his hand. A large crowd had amassed on the pavement below and watched as Fred approached the still befuddled-looking councillor who had tried to put a stop to the protest earlier that morning.

'This here,' Fred said as he thrust multiple sheets of paper directly under the councillor's bushy moustache, 'is a list of all the people who have signed our petition. Everyone who wants the common to stay. Who don't want your so-called luxury apartments.'

The councillor was speechless as he took hold of the document and glanced over it with a furious expression on his face. 'The decision's already been made,' he stated firmly. 'There's nothing you or I can do about it now.'

Just as the last vestige of Misty's hope had started to trickle away, Sheila pushed her way forward to the front of the crowd to join Fred. 'It's not that simple though, is it?' she persisted. 'You may have given official notice of the plans, but we still have time to file our objections. This is far from over yet.'

Ruby glanced proudly at her mother as the councillor stuttered before he turned his back on them and walked swiftly into the offices, slamming the door loudly behind him.

'That was great, Mum.' Ruby beamed. 'You really showed him who's boss.'

'I might have bought us a bit more time but there's still a lot to do if we want to really fight this.' Sheila grimaced.

'Thanks for coming,' Misty said gratefully. 'How did you know about the parade?'

'Ruby told me when she got home last night,' Sheila replied as she threw her daughter a smile. 'She explained everything to me, said you needed our help, and I was more than happy to oblige.'

'I wanted to do something to show you how sorry I am,' Ruby explained. 'I hope you can forgive me for being so selfish?'

Misty looked up at the sky as she pretended to consider Ruby's request. Without saying another word, she pulled Ruby into a tight embrace, and she knew that she had her best friend back where she belonged, by her side again.

Now that the show was over, the crowd had lost interest and dispersed back onto the high street below. Misty looked around keenly for a flash of golden hair in the crowd, but she could see no sign of the boy who claimed to be Sparkle's real owner.

'Are you ok?' Dylan asked as they mounted the horses and prepared to make their way home. They had chosen a quieter route back, feeling they had caused quite enough commotion for one day. After all the excitement of the parade, the noises of the horses and ponies seemed muffled, as if they were on mute.

'Remember I told you about the grey horse and the boy I saw when I first arrived in Redbridge?' Misty replied. 'Well, that was Sparkle and his real owner, who now wants him back.'

To her great relief, Dylan didn't say I told you so, but looked at Misty kindly as he positioned himself towards her. 'Perhaps he's just some silly kid who wants a free pony?' he said weakly.

'That's what Ruby said but I'm sure it was him I saw that day on the high street.'

'It does sound that way,' Dylan concurred. 'But whatever

happens, I promise I won't let him take Sparkle away from you.'

Misty wasn't sure there was anything Dylan could do to stop him if the mystery boy really was Sparkle's owner, but she appreciated his resolve. As they rode through the back streets of the city, she tried not to think that this could be one of her last ever rides on her favourite little grey pony.

After they had returned to the estate and released the horses back onto the common, Misty waited until everyone else had gone home and then went to find Sparkle at the top of the field. As she approached, the little pony whinnied softly in greeting as he raised his head and walked over to meet her.

'You were amazing today,' she told him. 'And I'm not angry with you about what happened with that boy. I know you were only saying hello.'

The pony nudged her hand tenderly, searching for treats as he nibbled on the sleeve of her jacket. Misty held out her empty hand and Sparkle snorted, his warm breath tickling her palm. It was as if he understood exactly what she was saying, although she hoped he wouldn't fully comprehend what she had to say next.

'And if you *do* belong to him, I'll let you go because I know how hard it is to be uprooted from everything and everyone you know and have to start over in a new place. If it's what you want, I'll give you up.'

When no treats had been forthcoming, Sparkle had gone back to grazing by Misty's side, but he lifted his head at the sound of her voice and observed her as she spoke.

'Goodnight, Sparkle,' she said as she walked away not turning her back on him but moving slowly so she could hold an image of him in her mind for ever. 'Thank you for everything.'

CHAPTER TWENTY-TWO

Misty spent most of the week lying low, constantly worrying that the mystery boy might turn up at any moment to take Sparkle away from her. By the following Monday morning, she was so concerned about going to school and leaving him untended that she almost decided to take another impromptu day off.

As she stumbled sleepily downstairs and fell into the kitchen, Misty noticed that her dad was already there waiting for her, further cementing the fact that there was no way she could get away with taking any more time away from school. It was the first week of the final half term and she had promised to help Ruby persuade her mum that she could go to the end-of-term disco, if Misty could manage to take her mind off Sparkle and his alleged owner for long enough to enjoy it.

Just as she was collecting her belongings to leave for the day, there was a sharp knock on the front door. Misty jumped sky high and spilt her tea clumsily over the table.

'You ok?' Dad asked, his brow furrowing. 'I wonder who on earth that could be?'

Before Misty could reply, her dad strolled leisurely to the front door and opened it cautiously; it *was* very early on a Monday morning to have uninvited visitors. Misty craned her head round the kitchen door so that she could see who it was. She could just make out Dylan's mum, Judy, and another woman about the same age as her that Misty thought looked familiar.

'Judy?' Misty's dad's voice rose in surprise. 'Is everything ok?'

'Can we come in?' she heard Judy reply.

'Of course.' Dad gestured towards the kitchen where Misty was still sat gawping at them. 'Come in, come in.'

The three adults tramped into the tiny room. They almost seemed like giants as they towered over Misty. There were only two chairs, so Misty's dad was forced to loiter by the work surface as Judy offered the other woman the remaining chair. Misty started to get up to give Judy her seat, but Judy put a firm hand on Misty's shoulder and wordlessly shook her head. Misty sat down again with a thud. Two mysterious appearances with only a week between them didn't bode well. The new woman looked apprehensively around the room, as if taking a mental photograph and then let out a long, shuddering sigh.

'I think you've met my son, Jim,' the woman ventured. 'And I'm his mum, Sarah.'

'Your son?' Misty asked.

Just when Misty thought things couldn't get any stranger, Sarah burst into tears. Judy put a comforting hand on her arm.

'Take your time,' Judy said. 'There's no rush.'

'It's very hard to explain,' Sarah stammered through her tears. 'I feel so guilty and ashamed. I should have known this would all end badly.'

'I think someone needs to explain what this is all about, and what it's got to do with my daughter, don't you?'

Misty smiled at her dad gratefully, but she was starting to think that she *did* have an inkling as to why they were here. 'Is this about Sparkle— I mean Silver?' she corrected when Sarah looked at her blankly. Misty noticed that the woman's golden hair was the exact same colour as her son's.

'It was Gary, my husband, who brought him here,' Sarah confessed. 'We knew he would be well looked after.'

'But Jim said he was stolen?' Misty exclaimed as slowly pieces of the puzzle were falling into place.

'They couldn't afford to keep him,' Judy explained as Sarah struggled to draw breath. 'So, they left the pony with us.'

'I told Judy that we'd left him here, so I knew someone was taking care of him. She told me what a good job you were doing, and I thought we would hear no more about it.'

Misty realised where she had seen this woman before. It was on the morning of the parade; she had been walking beside Judy and her father. 'But Jim must have been devastated?'

Misty knew how distraught she had felt at the prospect of Sparkle being taken away from her for good and she'd not been looking after him for long. She could only imagine how awful it must have been for Jim. 'You have to tell him,' she said firmly.

'We tried, but he wouldn't listen. He was adamant that Silver had been stolen and he was so angry that we let him believe it was true, it seemed easier than telling him that we had given him away.'

Misty could hardly believe what she was hearing. 'You *have* to tell him the truth.'

'I know,' Sarah replied. 'We should never have lied to him in the first place. He just jumped to the wrong conclusion, and it was easier not to correct him. We never should have done it. We should have realised he would find out eventually. He was so upset when he saw the pair of you together at the parade, I told him I'd come here and try to sort everything out.'

'I think we've heard enough, don't you?' Misty's dad interjected suddenly. 'Misty looks after that pony as if he's her own and I won't let you take him away from her. Even if I have to pay for the pony myself.'

Misty gasped. She knew they couldn't afford a pony; her dad didn't even have enough money to put food on the table at the minute.

'I'm sure that won't be necessary.' Judy tried her best to smooth things over. 'Sarah isn't saying they want the pony back—'

'But Jim does,' Misty interrupted. 'Jim's determined to get him back.'

'I know.' Sarah looked crestfallen. 'I don't know what to do.'

An idea was slowly forming in Misty's mind.

'I think I might have a suggestion...' Misty offered, though her heart strings were pulling in the opposite direction. 'You can't afford to keep Sparkle – I mean Silver – can you? Even if you wanted to?'

Sarah nodded her head in agreement as Judy looked at her quizzically. Misty took another deep breath.

'What if he was to stay here, in Redbridge, and Jim could help me look after him? We could share the responsibility. You wouldn't have to pay anything, but Jim would still have Silver in his life. Do you think that might work?'

'It's definitely worth a try, isn't it?' Judy urged. 'Once you've explained the situation to him, and been honest, perhaps he'll come round eventually.'

'Maybe.' Sarah looked doubtful, but she was resolved to give anything a try. 'Leave it with me.'

Misty's dad released his tight grip on the countertops. 'Well, if that's all sorted,' he said, looking pointedly at Misty. 'Don't you think it's about time you got yourself over to that school of yours?'

The rest of the week passed slowly, and by Thursday, when Misty still hadn't seen or heard anything from Jim or his mother, she started to feel lulled into a false sense of security. Ruby had kept both her and Jasmine busy with endless speculation about who would pair up with who at the end-of-term disco. Sheila had finally relented and said Ruby could attend, as long as Misty and Jasmine agreed to help her catch up with her maths and science over the summer holidays.

'It shouldn't be that bad,' Ruby relented. 'I've been practically locked in the library studying for weeks.'

The girls were busy adding the final touches to the signs they had made to advertise the disco. Glitter shimmered under the harsh strip lighting of the art room as they continued to discuss Ruby's latest predicament.

'I'm happy to help you,' Jasmine replied. 'Once the triathlon is out of the way, I'll have much more free time on my hands.'

After the parade was over, Jasmine had spent the remainder of the half-term holiday training hard every day. She had a gruelling regime which involved swimming, running and cycling each morning and Misty knew she was going to ace it.

'What about you, Misty?' Ruby asked.

'What about me?' Misty paused, her glue pen hovering questioningly over the sequin she was about to stick on.

'Isn't there anyone you like the look of in Year Ten and Eleven?'

'Not really,' Misty replied, blushing ever so slightly.

Ruby narrowed her eyes and focused her laser-sharp gaze on Misty's pink cheeks. Nothing ever got past her.

'It's that boy, isn't it?' she questioned, as she held up her finished poster with a flourish. 'The one I saw you with at the end of the parade. Not the one I had to rescue you from, the other one. The more attractive one.'

'His name's Dylan,' Jasmine offered quietly. 'They're just friends.'

'Right, and I'm the Queen of Sheba.' Ruby arched her eyebrow suspiciously. 'You must think I was born yesterday. I saw the way you were looking at him.'

Misty smiled but said nothing more about it. When the bell rang for the first lesson of the afternoon, she felt secretly relieved. As delighted as she was to have finally made up with Ruby, there were some things she wanted to keep to herself. This time, Misty wasn't lying to Ruby, she had promised never to conceal anything important from either of her best friends again, but some things were allowed to be kept private, and were best when they were held inside to be cherished.

That evening, as Misty was walking on autopilot towards the common, she pulled up with a start when she noticed the figure waiting for her by the gate. It wasn't Dylan, it was Jim, and Sparkle was standing with his head hanging over the gate beside him. It looked like they belonged together. She braced herself, expecting him to be angry, but instead he turned to her with a pensive smile.

'Mum told me how well you've taken care of him,' Jim said as he stroked Sparkle's neck. 'I'm sorry I got so angry at the parade. It was such a shock seeing the pair of you together. I really thought you'd stolen him.'

'I understand,' Misty said, as she made her way over to him. Sparkle gave her a friendly whinny in greeting. 'I didn't want to believe you, either.'

'So, you'll let me help you with him?' Jim shrugged, feigning nonchalance.

'Of course. He is really yours, after all.' Sparkle thrust his head towards her, wanting attention.

'He obviously likes you.' Jim laughed as the pony pushed his head into Misty's stomach. 'There is one thing though—'

'What's that?' Misty's insides ached, as she wondered if he'd had a change of heart.

'We can't call him Sparkle, it's way too girly.' Jim chuckled to himself.

Misty released some of the tension she was holding. On this point she was willing to back down, as long as she got to keep the sparkly, silver wonder pony in her life for good.

In all the excitement of the past week, she had almost forgotten what a very big *if* this still was, one that relied heavily on the council agreeing to leave the common alone. With Sheila's help, the community had lodged a formal objection and Fred was hoping they would hear back from the council soon.

CHAPTER TWENTY-THREE

Several weeks passed and still they heard nothing from the council. Misty still spent a lot of time looking after Silver, only now she had Jim to help her which also meant she could be a better friend to both Ruby and Jasmine. The only person who seemed uneasy about the new arrangement was Dylan, who grew increasingly distant from Misty the more time she spent with Jim and the two girls. But Misty was so ecstatic that she hadn't lost Silver completely that at first, she didn't notice his slow, silent retreat away from her.

Jim and Misty had originally planned to split taking care of Silver evenly, alternating the days they spent with him, but more and more often they found themselves looking after Silver together, bonded by their mutual love for the pony. Jim was a quiet and considerate boy, someone who seemed to think everything through carefully before he decided on the best course of action. Between them, Silver was getting five-star treatment, and Jim had taught Misty all of the pony's favourite things.

When Misty got to the common early one Saturday morning, Jim was already there methodically picking out Silver's feet. There was no sign of Dylan and the others. Although it was his turn to be with the pony, when Jim saw Misty approaching, he said, 'Why don't you ride him today?'

'That's ok, I'm happy to watch.' Misty was touched by his offer, but she knew how much she looked forward to her days with Silver and didn't want to deny Jim the same expectation. As she watched him ride Silver calmly around the field, she noticed what a good rider he was, how Silver responded seamlessly to his invisible commands. It was as if the boy and the pony were the same being, working as one towards the same outcome. Misty felt slightly envious but quickly wiped the feeling away. There was still so much she could learn from Jim and perhaps if they worked together, she would be as good a rider as he was one day.

'How do you do it?' Misty asked Jim, once he had dismounted and they were grooming Silver.

'Do what?' Jim asked, looking perplexed.

'Make all of it look so easy?' She gestured vaguely towards Silver and then to the common.

'Do I?'

'Yes, you make it look so effortless. Riding I mean,' Misty exclaimed. 'I wish I was as good as you.'

'You're a very good rider,' Jim replied. 'Especially considering how little experience you have.'

'I guess I'm just impatient. I want to be the best.'

Jim laughed. 'I'm definitely not *that* good.'

'Well, it seems that way to me,' Misty sighed as she tickled Silver under his chin, in the place Jim had taught her he liked best.

When they had finished grooming Silver and turned him back out onto the common, they could see Dylan and Carin making their way towards them.

When Dylan looked up and saw Jim and Misty together, his once open face seemed to shut down completely.

'What's wrong with you?' Carin asked him, waiting until they were within earshot of the others as if she deliberately wanted to embarrass him.

Dylan didn't reply but looked down at the dirt beneath him, doing his best to avoid eye contact with either Misty or Jim. Carin seemed to think better of teasing him, and instead made her way over to where Solo was waiting for her, leaving Misty, Dylan and Jim with a tense silence hanging in the air between them.

'Dylan—' Misty's voice trailed off when she saw the dark look on his face.

'I think I'll go and help Carin catch Solo,' Jim offered. 'See you later, Misty. Bye, Dylan.'

Misty watched aimlessly as Jim walked over to Carin.

She wanted more than anything for Dylan to warm to Jim the way she had done, to realise that he didn't have to worry, Jim wasn't going to take Silver away.

'He's nice once you get to know him,' Misty said hesitantly. 'Perhaps you could give him a chance?'

'I'd better go and get Colin,' Dylan replied awkwardly, all the usual humour leaving his voice. Gone was the easy-going boy with the joyful dance in his eyes and the light-hearted, infectious grin that Misty had come to rely on completely. Without them, she had no idea where to begin. Before she could reply, Dylan turned in the opposite direction.

'I'll see you around,' Dylan said abruptly as he walked towards the yard, leaving Misty standing along on the common with only her spinning mind left for company. She didn't understand why he was acting so strangely; she had reassured him that everything was fine. Perhaps he was still feeling anxious about the common, wondering what would happen to their home.

CHAPTER TWENTY-FOUR

As Misty and Jim's friendship grew stronger, Misty and Dylan were still circling each other from a distance, neither willing to admit how much they missed one another. Spring turned to summer and finally it was the last day of term and the evening of the school disco.

As they had no other dates, Ruby, Jasmine and Misty had agreed to spend the evening together. Festoon lighting covered the hall and a glitter ball hung in the centre, painting its walls in an array of sparkling colour. The sides of the room were lined with foldout tables covered in plates of sizzling sausage rolls and glasses of homemade fruit punch.

Ruby made quite an entrance, wearing her pink sequined Juliet dress from the play. Jasmine wore a demure blue velvet dress which complimented the colour of her eyes perfectly. Misty, who hadn't given the disco even a moment's thought until that morning, had hastily pulled out an old black dress from the back of the wardrobe, a long shapeless number that she had previously worn on Halloween as a witch's costume.

'What *are* you wearing?' Ruby said as soon as she clapped eyes on Misty.

'It's the only thing I could find,' mumbled Misty defensively, she was much more at home in jeans, trainers and a t-shirt.

'Well, I suppose it will have to do then. It's a good job you're not trying to impress anyone.'

By now the girls had walked over to the buffet and were shifting their weight aimlessly from foot to foot, as they watched their classmates take to the dancefloor uncertainly. Mr Groves, the maths teacher, was manning the music and seemed to have chosen a Spotify playlist from some time in the previous century. Everyone burst into laughter as Madonna's *Like a Virgin* burst out of the stereo to be quickly skipped over and replaced with Abba's *Dancing Queen*.

Can't someone do something about the music?' Ruby complained loudly and went to request something more recent.

'Is everything ok?' Jasmine asked Misty, once Ruby was out of earshot. 'With Silver, and the common and everything, I mean. Have you heard anything?'

'Not yet,' Misty replied. 'And I still haven't spoken to Dylan.'

Misty had told the girls how oddly Dylan had been behaving ever since Jim's arrival. Ruby thought he was probably just jealous, but Jasmine wondered if there might be slightly more to it than that.

'Maybe you need to make the first move,' Jasmine suggested, raising her voice over the cheers and laughter.

Ruby shimmied over, music now sorted, and pulled both of her friends onto the dancefloor. 'Come on, let's dance!'

Misty tried her best to enjoy the party, but her mind was elsewhere. After speaking to Jasmine, she wanted to go home and in her heart of hearts, she knew that most of all she wanted to see Dylan.

'I've got to go,' she announced. 'There's somewhere else I should be.'

Ruby looked perplexed for a moment but instead of getting annoyed she took a deep breath. 'Go get that handsome freckle boy,' she said mischievously. 'We all know that's the real reason you're leaving.'

Misty laughed and reached out to hug Jasmine, saying her goodbyes as she did so. As she left the hall, her pace quickened and before she knew it, she was running towards the bus stop, towards home.

But when Misty finally arrived back in Redbridge, it wasn't Dylan she raced off in search of. Instead, she turned left and ran in the opposite direction from the dark common and down the street towards home.

'Dad, are you in?' she shouted, bursting through the door. As she entered the living room, she noticed that it was in fact full to the brim with people. Her dad was standing by the front window with a glass in his hand talking to Fred, and Dylan was squashed onto their old sofa with Judy, Carin and Bethany. Even Ruby's mum Sheila was there, talking to Jasmine's parents.

'What's going on? What are you all doing here?'

'We've having a celebration,' her dad grinned. 'A double celebration in fact.'

'What? Why?' Misty struggled for words. 'Have we heard back from the council?'

'We've only gone and done it.' Dylan brandished a letter under her nose, his previous standoffishness temporarily forgotten. The familiar council letterhead floated across the top of the page.

'That's those eejits told,' Carin said bluntly, causing Judy to raise her eyebrows in disapproval at her daughter's colourful choice of words.

'For now, at least,' Fred warned. 'They say it's only temporary while they consider what to do next.'

'They're probably busy trying to work out how they can sell it from under our noses,' Dylan replied. 'But we've won, that's what matters.'

Misty wasn't sure it was all that mattered but at least it gave them some more time to figure out what to do next. And Silver and the others would get to keep their home for the time being.

'What happens now?' Misty asked.

'We've been given six months to come up with enough evidence to overthrow the plans for good, to prove that the common provides a vital green space for the local community,' Fred explained. 'The letter says that the building work is temporarily on hold while they consider our appeal.'

'You said it was a double celebration?' Misty asked hopefully, suddenly remembering that her dad was due to hear back from his job application by the end of the term.

Her dad's grin broadened up to his ears. 'I finally heard back from the school. I got the job!' he spat out jubilantly. 'Start after the summer holidays.'

'That's amazing news,' Misty replied, but she felt her heart sink when she looked towards Dylan. 'Will we be moving back then?'

There was a pause as her dad looked at her thoughtfully as if he was balancing an invisible seesaw in his mind. Misty held her breath and wondered what he was going to say next. Luckily, she didn't have to wait for long.

'I thought we might stay here,' Dad said, gesturing to all of their new friends. 'We seem to have settled in ok, don't you think? Would be a shame to have to move all over again.'

'I think...' Misty paused for a second, looking nervously towards Dylan. 'I think... that's the best piece of news I've heard all day.'

Misty had agreed to meet Dylan down at the common first thing the following morning. She couldn't help feeling edgy as it was the first time he had asked her to meet him since Jim had started to come to Redbridge. She didn't want to get her hopes up, but she was secretly wishing his invitation meant that their relationship would start to improve again.

She also couldn't wait to share the news with Silver and Colin that they were going to be able to stay on the common for now. She had no doubt that the horses would be able to understand them. As Misty strode purposefully down the hill, she could see Dylan waiting for her at the gate. Her heart flipped over as she took in the scene in front of her.

'All right?' Dylan nodded his head in greeting.

'I'm good,' Misty replied, feeling the new awkwardness that seemed to cling in the air between them.

For once Dylan seemed lost for words, then he laughed uneasily. 'I hope you won't replace me completely, now you've met Jim.'

'Is that why you've been avoiding me?' Misty asked. 'I know things are a bit different now.'

'I was... a tiny bit jealous... there, I've admitted it.' Dylan stopped abruptly and Misty felt as if his eyes were looking directly through hers and straight into her soul. Suddenly, she was aware of his arm pressing against hers, which felt as if it might burst into flames. He tilted towards her and, so fast that she thought she might have imagined it, he planted a small heartfelt kiss on her cheek. She felt herself begin to blush.

Then, as if nothing had happened, Dylan jumped over the fence and began to run towards the horses who were grazing peacefully in the field in front of them. 'Shall we go for a ride?' he called back to her. He was grinning wildly, his arms outstretched as if to catch her.

'That sounds nice,' Misty replied, vaulting the fence in one swift motion, and making her way towards Dylan, her newest, oldest, and greatest of friends.

'I would never replace you,' she whispered, so softly that he wouldn't be able to hear her through the morning breeze.

Misty's hair whipped silently over her face as she raced Dylan across the beach, Silver's hooves thudding furiously over the sand beneath her. She could hear the heavier plod of Colin as he lumbered behind them, now struggling to keep up with Silver's nimbler stride.

'It's not fair,' Dylan grumbled as they pulled up at the other end of the cove. 'I can never keep up with the two of you these days. I need to find myself a speedier steed.'

As much as Dylan complained Misty knew he would never give up on Colin, whom he was just as fond of as she was of Silver. Jim was busy today, so they were making the most of having an entire day alone with the horses, doing their favourite thing, racing across the beach.

'Come on,' Misty shouted. 'I'll race you to the other side.'

She was already galloping away from him by the time Dylan had a chance to register her words. She hunched low over Silver's back, urging him on, faster and faster across the sand. There was no room for fear, girl and pony were one as they moved rapidly towards the shore. When they reached the water's edge, Silver lifted his knees high as the icy water tickled at his feet. He pranced excitedly though the waves, his neck arched proudly as he snorted in surprise.

'Good boy.' Misty took hold of his mane and pressed him further into the water. As they left the shallows, Silver plunged about frantically before launching himself out into the sea. 'That's it,' Misty gasped. 'You can do it. You're swimming.'

She turned back to face the beach. Dylan's hand was covering his eyes as he watched her from the safety of the shore. There was no way a horse as cumbersome as

Colin was going to be persuaded to go swimming. Misty waved and made her way slowly back towards them. Her trainers and leggings were soaking, and she shivered in the warmth of the early morning sun. It was the first day of the school holidays, the middle of summer, but the sea was always freezing.

'I didn't know he could swim,' Dylan remarked once Misty and Silver were within earshot.

'This pony can do anything,' Misty replied, smiling to herself as she reached forward and scratched Silver behind the ear.

'Weren't you scared?' he asked.

Misty cocked her head to one side as she thought of how she could best phrase her answer.

'Not really, no,' she replied. 'I had the best teacher.'

EPILOGUE

The fences that lined the edges of the common were covered in banners and placards, remnants from the parade which served as a constant reminder of everything that the people of Redbridge still had to lose. The common was safe for now, but the threat of the developers was never far away and the fight was far from over, it had just paused as if to let out a pregnant sigh before summoning the energy to start all over again.

Misty had been with Ruby and Jasmine making plans for the new school year. As much as she'd enjoyed a summer of riding on the beach and hanging out with Dylan, Jim and Carin, she was looking forward to seeing her other friends every day too. It was Ruby's birthday at the beginning of September, and she had asked them to help her plan a massive party.

It was a warm, dry evening in late August and Misty was on her way to meet Dylan in their usual spot by the gate to the common, so that she could say goodbye. The sky was bright and clear of cloud, full of the optimism of a fresh beginning. At the start of the summer, Dylan had been offered a place on an apprenticeship at a local racing yard and would be leaving the following morning. Although it wasn't far from home, he would be living on site and Misty would no longer be able to see him every single day.

With all the worry about losing the common and then Silver, she had never imagined for a second that it would be Dylan she was going to be saying goodbye to. As sad as she was to see him go, Misty knew he would come back to visit her and Colin as often as he was able to, and although it was bittersweet, she didn't want him to see how upset she really was in case it put him off going altogether.

'Misty,' Dylan said as she approached, his once unreadable eyes brimming with emotion.

'Dylan,' Misty echoed, feeling oddly formal and unsure of herself now that she was there beside him.

Before she could think of something meaningful to say, Dylan reached out and hugged her. He held her tightly and their embrace seemed to sum up everything that was left unsaid, floating in the ether between them. As the sun began to set, they sat together watching the horses grazing peacefully on the hillside, content just to be in each other's company, not saying a word.

'I don't want to say goodbye, Dylan,' Misty confessed.

'Neither do I,' Dylan replied. 'But maybe we don't have to. Say goodbye, I mean.'

'I'll see you soon?' Misty suggested.

'Exactly. I'll see you soon. I'll see you very soon.' Dylan grinned. 'Next weekend, in fact.'

He nudged her arm playfully and the tension between them instantly melted away. As the sky darkened and Misty walked in the dusky shadows back to her home, she knew Dylan would keep his promise, and that they would be together again soon, riding through the waves on their favourite beach, the ghosts of the past firmly behind them.

ACKNOWLEDGEMENTS

I'm forever grateful to all the people and ponies at the Wormwood Scrubs Pony Centre for giving me a safe haven and home away from home from the ages of eight to eighteen.

This book is a heartfelt ode to all the pony books I devoured ferociously as a child. A special mention goes out to Patricia Leach's *Jinny at Finmory* series, which proves that a great story really can transcend time and on whose protagonist I based Misty's fiery red hair.

City of Horses took inspiration from various urban equestrian communities in the UK and Ireland, including the Penlan Estate in Swansea and Dublin's O'Devaney Gardens. Thanks to Marion Bergin's documentary *Saoirse* and the BBC's *The City of Horses* for offering additional insight into this unique and vibrant way of life.

Dad, thank you for the lifts, the 7am doughnuts and the endless yard sweeping when I was too young to be left at the stables alone. Thanks to Kathy Heaps for always sneaking me into a lesson somehow. Thanks to Cheyenne for making all my horse-shaped dreams a reality, you will always hold such a special place in my heart.

As ever thank you to everyone who has helped make this book a reality. Sarah, thank you for helping to polish the words on every page until they Sparkle. All at Pushkin and Bounce, and all the booksellers, reviewers, teachers and librarians who have supported me along the way so far. Thanks, Thy, for another knockout cover, I'm lucky to have you not only as a designer, but as a friend.

Lastly, thank you, Greg, for making the good times shine even more brightly and the bad times lose their darkness.

Also by this author...

THE MYSTERY OF THE MISSING MUM

FRANCES MOLONEY

PUSHKIN CHILDREN'S

'A heartfelt story told with such passion and authenticity it will stick with you as though it was a memory of your very own'

NADINE WILD-PALMER